HARSU & THE WERESTOAT

HARSU
& THE
WERESTOAT

BARBARA ELSE

GECKO PRESS

CONTENTS

Part Three: The Perfect Child

Part Four: Time & Stone

PART ONE

THE LOOKING-CAKE

GOOD-MEATS & SWEET-MEATS

EXCEPT FOR FIVE GODLET-DROPS THAT RAN IN HIS blood, Harsu was human. He was a long-legged boy who would soon be a man, and had a small room in his mother's palace. Every day he missed his father. But the godlet-drops kept him strong inside where it counts most.

His mother might look like a woman but she was Daama, the forty-first daughter of the fifty-ninth daughter of one of the Wind God's nine thousand or so children.

Before Harsu was six she'd taught him about the universe: it was a plate covered by a dome, and the dome was the sky. Up there lived many relatives: demi-gods or that sort of thing—great-grandfathers, very-great-grandmothers, aunts, uncles and cousins. Others roved where they wanted over the plate of the universe. With paws they dug deep in mountains, or with flippers and fins swam in the great river Euphrates. A few were as tall and warty as a pine tree, some tinier than a whisker on the chin of a bee.

When Harsu turned six, his father started teaching him too. He was a warrior-physician, human right down to his toenails. "Now here is my real strength. Watch and learn," he said. "This is a clay lentil."

In one hand his father held a damp piece of clay which he'd shaped into a rectangle. In the other hand was a stylus split from a reed. With deft little movements Harsu's father pressed the stylus several times into the clay. It made a group of small lines and triangles.

"This first sign is the sound of your name." It looked like trees with pointed tops.

"This next set means *my*—this one is *son*," his father continued. He spoke the sounds that went with each sign. "I'm writing *Harsu my son the figh-ter.* That is line one. This next line is, *patience is bravery.* Now, *wits are the best sickle-sword.*"

It had seemed interesting but difficult.

However, on the student's side of the clay lentil Harsu pressed a clumsy copy of the markings for his own name and *my son.*

"Well done. Enough for now." His father covered the lentil with a wet cloth to keep it soft for tomorrow.

But next day a fever struck Harsu. For days he sweated with dreams. His mother Daama screamed with anger. His father answered her for a long time in a deep gentle voice, then more loudly. As Harsu's fever-dreams grew worse, his skin broke out in a terrible rash. Daama screamed again.

"I am saving his life," his father said.

"He's my perfect child, my only child," his mother shouted. "I will not have him scarred!"

"Whatever happens he'll be your child!" his father roared.

The storm of their arguing moved from the bedside while fever burned in Harsu's head. It was important to tell his mother, *I love you too.* He struggled from bed and collapsed on the floor. He heard a rage-hiss like a stoat, and the wailing of slaves. His father rushed in and spoke more words while he wrote on the lentil. But they made no sense through Harsu's headache. Daama shrieked. The air was busy with whirling dust. Then the air split again with the sound of a werestoat that bounded up the walls of his room, screaming with fury and triumph.

The fever-dreams broke into fragments. Harsu felt a cool cloth in the hands of a servant. She was pressing it to his face, soothing and comforting.

When at last Harsu woke properly, his father was gone from the palace.

In the six years since, Harsu had been patient, as his father had written. The servants and slaves treated him kindly. It didn't take a clever boy to know when was best to keep out of his mother's way. It was certainly wise never to ask about his warrior father.

—

All morning thirty servants and five cooks had worked at the seven ovens. Twenty slaves had swept all twenty patios. The mistress-princess was going nowhere, but yet another ten slaves had polished every bell on Daama's seventy carts and carriages. They'd buffed the hooves of all the onagers whose job it was to pull them. From down in the field came their horsey snorting that sounded like the last part of their names, *dgerr.*

Rattling down the drive came wicker carts laden with guests and pulled by donkeys, or onagers if the guests could afford them. Men or women, they wore rich linen drapery and their wigs were heavy with curls. They brought gifts for Mistress-princess Daama, who was plump and smiling in new finery.

It was time Harsu made himself scarce.

He ran over three patios, past two fountains to the palace kitchen.

Slaves scurried in, pushing past him and the Chief Cook to hide themselves in nooks and cupboards.

Harsu rolled his eyes. "What a shame there was no time to polish the drops of water in every fountain."

"You have your father's sense of humour, long-legs," the Chief Cook muttered. "For his sake, be careful." With a muscly arm he pointed to a platter. "Hurry, feed yourself."

Harsu grabbed a skewer of grasshoppers and took a bite. "Thank you. It smells so good. Tastes even better."

The Chief Cook gave a mock bow as he would have to Harsu's father in the days when they camped before battle.

Harsu began filling a basket to take to the field. "Did you and my father have to remind each other that patience is courage? It grows painful."

"I know today is worse." The Chief Cook gave a smile of sympathy. "But just a few more months and you'll be a man."

The air swelled with the visitors' laughter. Music from stringed instruments rose from the fanciest patio. Processions of servants offered marble plates piled with good-meats and sweet-meats.

"How naughty, I shouldn't!" the guests cried. Their jewels clattered when they seized the treats anyway.

The Chief Cook tapped Harsu's arm. "Don't hang about."

The man was right. Already the visitors had started to chant.

"We are awash with jealous tears. Daama's new babies are perfect. So glossy, fatter than fruit. Their cheeks are dewy, smoother than the finest linen."

Harsu shrugged a shoulder to hide the old fever-scars down the left side of his face. He grabbed another skewer of grasshoppers and sprinted to the onagers' field.

But the guests chanted louder. Harsu heard all the words even here.

"Daama's grief at having no child of her own has been a long torment."

The strongest onager, his father's old war-steed, paced over to Harsu and snorted. *Dgerr.*

"I don't care. They can't change the truth," Harsu said. "I'm her son, her only true child. I'm just not perfect."

"She's the most excellent mother in all the universe. She deserves these gorgeous babies," bellowed the guests.

It had been like this the first time Daama stole a new baby. But this time was worse. She'd stolen twins.

HOW ILLOGICAL

IT WAS HOURS BEFORE THE GUESTS LEFT, BURPING AFTER too many sweet-meats. In moments, Harsu heard the stolen twins beginning to cry.

He elbowed the war-steed onager and spoke in a high baby-voice. *"Waah, somebody pooed in my botty-cloth."*

Daama's screams and shouts rang down to the field. A gaggle of servants ran into the house, many others came hurrying out. The babies' cries became piercing. Daama shrieked, more furious still. A flock of birds soared overhead as if they sped from an enemy.

Dgerr. The onager nudged Harsu now and made him glance over his shoulder. Every onager was bowing its head at two people approaching. A man and woman. Their toes only grazed the tips of the grass and their garments floated. They weren't wearing curly wigs but they looked wealthy. The man had straight moon-silver hair. The woman's hair was silver curls on one side and straight black on the other.

9

They were relatives. There would be trouble.

Harsu stood as straight as he could.

Through a frown, the woman smiled at him. Her gaze was deep brown with no whites showing, like the eyes of a fox. The man's eyes were the colour of the blue roller bird, his eyebrows feathery.

The woman beckoned Harsu to come with them to the palace. His father's onager paced behind him.

As they came near, Daama rushed out to a patio, still yelling and screaming. The man raised a hand. She fell silent so fast a bung might have been stuck in her gullet.

The man lifted both arms like a cradle. Somehow one of the babies appeared there, eyes round with surprise. The woman lifted her arms, and in them lay the other baby blowing bubbles.

"Daama," the man said. "Once again you've broken your promise."

"We warned you there must be no more babies stolen and harmed," the woman said.

"Harmed?" Daama widened her eyes. "But how illogical. These babies are perfect."

"You have no idea how to care for them." The woman mimicked the visitors: *"Oh Daama, how hard it is for you to be a new mother.* You didn't even have the babies yourself, you stole them. You were an uncivilised horror when you were small. When we threw you out, not one of us thought it possible you could grow worse. But you have. All you do is think of yourself and fatten on sympathy and praise you never deserve."

"If that's what you think, then take the babies," shouted Daama.

"We certainly will, as we did last time. They'll go right back to their parents. Don't steal any more," said the man. "And this time we're taking Harsu as well."

Harsu's mother stuck her chin in the air. "You have no right. He's not yours. And he's not harmed."

The way the woman looked at Daama made Harsu think of a sickle-sword. But her words were quiet. "There are many ways to harm a child. All children should have a parent who talks to them and plays with them. All children should have the comfort of a barley cake prepared by someone who loves them."

"Each child should have the warmest cloak in all the universe," added the man.

Daama scoffed. "As if more than one cloak could be the warmest."

The woman raised a hand. For a second time Daama fell silent.

Interesting. But, after all, Harsu should be fair, as his father always had been. And Daama was his mother. So he spoke up.

"Esteemed relatives, of course my mother talks to me

when she's not busy. I play with the onagers. The Cook feeds me well. And I have a cloak."

The onager gave a snort. Harsu's only cloak was so short by now it hardly covered his backside.

The man jiggled the baby. "Harsu, you were stubborn like this six years ago. We should have whisked you away then. We were wrong to have listened to this creature's promises. Come with us now."

Daama grabbed Harsu. "Tell your great-great-uncle and grand-great-aunt you refuse to leave. Any mother has to be admired for having a loyal son."

She didn't admire him though. Harsu's hand lifted to cover the scars marking his cheek from chin to his lashes.

For a moment Daama squeezed her eyes shut. Then she cried, "I will not be left with nothing. Your father was at least known for his loyalty."

The onager snorted again behind Harsu as if to say, *And how did that help him?*

But Harsu put his shoulders back and bowed to the relatives. "Thank you for your concern. I have no father and that is always grief to me. But I still have a mother. All children owe respect to the one who bore them."

The aunt's sharp look was on him now. "For most children that is certainly true."

Harsu stood tall. "I'm the son of a warrior-physician, a leader. And after all, I'll soon be a man."

His mother's hand flew to her heart.

The great-great-uncle sighed.

The grand-great-aunt cupped Harsu's scarred cheek. Between them, the baby gurgled. Its little hand rested on him too.

Then the aunt's fox-brown eyes scanned the estate and lingered on a thicket just past the onagers' field. Still stroking his cheek, she spoke to Harsu. "Your human father was the best of men, brave, clever and kind. Remember, you're the best of boys."

In his heart the godlet-drops simmered.

The onager nudged the grand-great-aunt. She whispered to it. It nudged her again. She was so gentle Harsu almost changed his mind. But no. He had decided.

The man bounced the twin in his arms and sniffed its botty-cloth. *"Phou.* High time someone had a freshen-up."

The relatives looked a last time at Daama, who kept her mouth tight. With extra attention they stared at her chin and hands, the human-smooth skin.

"We will know if you break your promise," the aunt said. "And you must keep that woman shape. We will know if you let it drop."

Harsu nearly changed his mind again. But he stood steady.

With the stolen twins safe in their arms, the aunt and uncle glided away.

SQUASHED FIGS

T HE MOMENT THE RELATIVES WERE OUT OF SIGHT, Daama looked Harsu up and down. "Every boy creates a quagmire of bedevilment."

If that's what she thought, how come she wanted to keep him? Harsu had never figured his mother out.

She paced around the patio. "Where in the universe do those two expect me to find a cloak at a moment's notice? It isn't possible."

A young servant stumbled out of the palace as if someone had shoved her. "Mistress-princess," she stammered, "three hundred cloaks hang in the seventh wardrobe. This very day f-five of the guests brought new cloaks for you."

Daama's teeth bit together and she spoke through them. "Foolish girl. This daughter of a daughter of a child of the Wind God never shares. The cloaks are mine. They'll be mine forever."

"If I may, Mistress-princess?"

It was the Chief Cook with a folded cloak over an arm.

The girl hurried away. Daama's eyes narrowed as she stared at the cloak. But she said nothing.

The Cook bowed to her, then smiled at Harsu.

"I've kept this in my old travel trunk for many years. If you want it, it is yours."

His mother didn't say thanks, but Harsu did. He swung the cloak around his shoulders to see how it felt. It had a handy inner pouch for snacks or trinkets. It was also edged with copper tokens, discs that chimed now and then when the cloak moved. That might be why the Cook didn't mind handing it on. It might also be why Daama seemed to sneer at it. But it was warm. Even if Harsu grew as tall as his warrior father was in his memory, it would always be big enough.

"Oh—thank you too, noble mother," he remembered to say, though she'd had nothing to do with it. "Your kindness puts the grace in gracious."

Her scowl changed to a smile. "The boy flatters me! A feast! He and I must have a feast."

The cooks and servants rushed off to rustle up some leftover nibbles.

Daama started singing a song about a donkey who tried to drink the entire Euphrates River. Harsu remembered it from years ago when he was little and his father was alive. It had made them all scream with laughter then. He was too old for that now and just concentrated on not tripping up while he danced beside her, swinging the cloak. He wanted to ask about his father but it would not be wise to push his luck.

After three days of dancing and song his mother was no longer as plump as his grand-great-aunt had said she was.

It would be disastrous if she grew unhappy.

Harsu washed his face and hands in an earthenware bowl and ran his fingers through his tangled black hair. In a copper mirror he practised pulling the cloak up to hide his scars. His father had been handsome. Mind you, Harsu was fairly certain all boys believed that of their fathers. They would all have hopes of their mothers too.

He found Daama in the palace reception room, on her finest throne with the comfortable cushion. A few flies buzzed. Scattered around were scarves and jewels, boxes of precious stone, and a bronze plate heaped with stuffed figs. On her head was her newest headdress with the gold lily coronet.

The discs on his cloak chimed and made her startle.

He bowed and smiled. "Mother, I'm here to support you. I'm very close now to being a man ... "

"What use is that?" She flung the plate. It clanged off the wall and drummed around. "A grown-up child who will leave me! And if he doesn't leave, how can I ever show him to my guests anyway?"

"When I grow a beard, Mother ..."

"No beard will ever cover all of it. Never." She leapt up and stamped on a fig. "Never." On she went, *stamp*, *never*, in a dance of rage. Her nose turned sharp and snouty. Fur sprouted on the backs of her hands. Fur covered her cheeks and chin.

Harsu felt as if his blood drained out of him. He realised that deep inside he'd known since he was ill. It wasn't all fever-dreams. Daama, his mother, was a werestoat.

This was what the relatives meant. The grand-great-aunt had warned Daama it must not happen again: no stealing babies and no changing from her human shape.

Harsu backed out of the throne room and bumped into the Chief Cook.

"I don't want to talk about it. I am going to be with the onagers." Harsu could hardly believe how strong his own voice was. "Just leave her be."

Harsu was still in the field next morning when he glimpsed Daama at a palace door. She was in human shape, dressed like a perfect mistress-princess. The relatives wouldn't have noticed she'd broken her promise just for a moment. But she must have known she'd taken a risk.

She disappeared back inside. But he thought he'd wait in the field to make sure she calmed down properly. It would be best right now if she didn't see him. But his scars didn't matter to anyone else because most people had a wart or a lopsided smile or an ear that stuck out. And she must know she'd been illogical, that he couldn't stay a boy forever.

However, as the day went on, more and more she hissed at the gardeners and the slave-child who scooped dead insects out of the fountains. She screeched at cooks, maids, the slave who polished the wheels of the carts. She beat the one who made the clay tablets for writing messages, lists and instructions.

Even at this distance Harsu's eardrums felt sliced up and danced on. The onagers all backed away to the furthest fence.

He stayed that night with the onagers too. The palace echoed with banging and crashing, chirrups of rage, the screams of a mean-tempered animal.

As soon as the sun rose, all the servants fled with their bags packed.

"Sorry," the Chief Cook called to Harsu. "I've had enough. I'm only human. Good luck, be strong. You know your father was my dearest friend. The cloak was his. Look in the third oven."

Before the next hour was up, all thirty slaves scrambled from the palace as well. "She gnaws with the jaws of vanity," cried one.

"She grips with the talons of spite," another wailed.

"I'd rather starve in the wilderness," wept a third.

And they were gone.

Harsu let himself take five deep breaths into the folds of the cloak. All this was because he, Daama's only child, wasn't perfect, and she was not allowed to steal more babies to make up for it. It was not a sensible explanation, but she wasn't sensible either. She was Daama.

He straightened up. For a moment he hoped the relatives would come back. But just for a moment. He wasn't a baby.

No sound came from the palace. His mother would be remembering she had to be civilised. He wouldn't interrupt.

He was hungry, though, so he snuck to the kitchen. All he found in the cold third oven was a pottery tablet, just a student's lentil, not newly baked but hardened years ago to make the signs on it permanent. What use was that? The Cook knew Harsu had never been taught to read and write.

He chucked it into a corner and it broke in half.

Back in the fields he picked a cob from the corn that was growing there. He peeled back the leaves. It was just about ripe, so he picked more and shared some with the onagers. The war-steed held the cobs under its hooves and used its teeth to rip the leaves off for itself.

What a clever creature. Harsu laughed.

Then to pass time he examined every thread of the cloak, ran his thumb over the copper tokens and felt the markings stamped into them. He wished he could read. They'd be warrior symbols and physician's charms, little mementos of his father.

On the second day black smoke billowed from the kitchen chimney. Curly as a wig, it descended over the estate. Harsu's nose ran and the animals snorted.

After a week a *boom!* filled the air and flames shot out the chimney. The hissing screams sounded again and continued throughout the night.

The morning was silent.

Harsu edged closer. There was no sign of his mother. On the inside of the kitchen door he found deep scratches from iron-hard claws the right size for a stoat.

But the biggest oven was roaring. The pantry shelves were crammed with meat, fresh fruit and vegetables, and dried produce of all kinds. Cooking! Daama must be managing it with the enchantments she'd learned among the demi-gods when she was young. She wasn't doing very well yet. But if the relatives came back, they would see she was making serious efforts to be civilised.

The broken pottery lentil still lay in the corner where Harsu had tossed it. Maybe the Cook had saved it because it was the one his father had written on, trying to teach him? Probably not. But he gathered it up and loped back to the field where he could study it.

He fitted it together. There were four lines of signs, three made tidily. The last one looked rushed. On the other side, the student had written only one line. Even Harsu could see it was uneven and clumsy. Could it be his own try at writing? If so, it would say *Harsu my son.*

He decided he may as well stuff the pieces in the pouch of his father's cloak.

FIRST CAKE IN THE UNIVERSE

OVER THE NEXT DAYS THE CHIMNEY-BILLOWS TURNED from stinking black to mottled grey with a whiff of sweetness. At last there were only shimmers of heat against a blue sky.

Harsu heard Daama call him. He jogged to the main patio.

Her cheeks were plump again, rosy and smooth. She wore a new shawl which she must have conjured by the same magic that stocked the pantry. A new black headdress was studded with rubies. It resembled a giant reverse-ladybird. Harsu kept that thought to himself.

She held a small dish with a lid and beckoned him close. "No sign of a beard. Open up." On his tongue she popped a pellet. It tasted like the preservative used to make bottle stoppers. It dissolved before he could spit it out.

"*Eugh*, what—"

"Just follow me." She led him to the great reception room.

On a table sat a plate that held something round, as big as Harsu's head but flat on top. It smelled like honey and glistened with glaze.

"Behold," she said. "I've exerted myself beyond belief. I'm the first woman in the universe to make this creation."

"What is it?" asked Harsu.

Her face grew plumper. "I've baked figs and raisins, nuts and dates together into this stately shape. It is a *cake* bigger and better than any other has ever been. Admire."

"It is beyond splendid," he said. "What is it for?"

She smiled. "It is to celebrate a grand occasion or special person. For example, an excellent mother would bake such a treat for the birthday of the perfect child whom she loved beyond measure."

Harsu felt his face burn. Was today his birthday? Did she mean she loved him?

"What would someone do in the celebration?" he asked.

She smiled again and folded her hands. "Beside the plate lie the knife of celebration and the gold server. The birthday person would cut the cake while everyone else sang a joyful chant with words of good wishes."

His face burned even more. Good wishes. For him. He reached for the knife.

Daama snatched it first. "An invention by the daughter of the daughter of an important god's daughter must not be destroyed. This creation is only for looking."

Harsu kept expression off his face. After all, this was the first celebration cake in the universe. Of course it was special. And for many weeks nobody had visited to praise her. He'd better do it himself.

"Amazing Mother," he said. "Magnificent is too mild a description for your triumph with this superb success."

She stood smiling at the cake.

And ... oh well, that seemed to be it.

The awful taste of the black pellet lingered. Harsu snaffled a handful of dates from a side table and ran back to the field on his lanky legs. He held his hand flat and offered a date to his father's onager.

"It sticks to your teeth," he warned. "But at least it's a good taste."

PICNIC OF PASTRIES

L ONG DAYS PASSED. HARSU DIDN'T LOOK AT THE pottery lentil, there was no point. It was more fun to ride bareback on his father's war-steed and play with the young onagers.

One afternoon Daama called him again. She waited on the grandest patio in another rich headdress and another new cloak. Her smile was excited. Beside her was a basket piled with honey-pastries.

In her hand was a spinning-top of heavy wood carved like a paw. A faint hum like a thousand wasps seemed to seep from it. It was older than anything Harsu had seen in all his twelve years—thirteen if it had been his birthday when she made the cake.

So he might be only a whisker away now from being a man. His hand went to his chin. Not even the least fluff.

"Stop messing about," Daama said. "Bring the basket and don't nibble." She marched for the gate.

Harsu started to smile. A picnic, like ordinary human mothers had with their sons. His father had been right. All he'd had to do was let time pass, be patient and tolerant.

On the long walk to the road beside the river no one else was about. The basket grew heavy even though it was only pastries. At last Harsu stole a crumb. So good! Even if it left an odd after-tang.

Then ahead on the riverbank stood a boy, maybe seven years old. He wore a copper headband on sleek black hair. His kilt had a rich fringe, his chest was bare. The boy raised his arms and began a chant. Two grown-ups sat watching— the boy's parents. In front of them, fruit and barley cakes lay on a blanket.

"Stay out of sight." Daama thrust Harsu behind a thorn bush—*ow!* She grabbed the basket and hid herself behind an acacia tree.

Harsu's human blood and the godlet-drops began churning with unease.

The boy sang more loudly. *"I am Zamuna, I boast of my deeds. I am the most excellent runner since the first day of the universe."*

Harsu took such a gasp he had to spit out a fly. It was "The Ode of Praise to the King" but the little boaster was using his own name.

"Even sun and moon hide their faces in shame because I'm so good-looking," chanted the boy.

"You are adorable, my Zamuna, my handsome honey-star," cried the mother.

The father applauded. "My son is so good at running he upsets the wind. It's so ashamed of its weakness that it hides away up the butcher's butt-crack."

Daama stepped into view with her basket. "Does a sensible mother allow a child to boast to these extremes?" she said. "Does a wise father encourage such a bragger?" She tossed a pastry to each of them. "Eat."

"What ..." the father began.

Arm raised high, Daama drew loops in the air. The parents sat as if tied with invisible ropes while the pastries rushed to stuff themselves into their mouths.

The little boy tried to run to his mother. But Daama produced the wooden top. It whirred around Zamuna and sent out a trace of something sweet and sickening. The child teetered on tiptoes.

She held the basket under his nose and began to croon. "I am alone, trampled with sorrow. I have no husband. My beautiful children are gone, every one of them ripped away from my loving arms. But here you stand, so handsome, Zamuna. Come with me."

She jiggled the basket and stepped away. "No ordinary father or mother should have a child like you. And parents who puff up their child's importance are criminal and ridiculous, a blot on the universe. I need the perfect child to praise me as I deserve." Daama's voice was purring now. "Then all my guests will admire me for having you."

The parents struggled and choked.

But the spinning-top moved to and fro behind the boy, pushing him to follow Daama, his eyes almost as glazed as the pastries.

Harsu couldn't move. She'd promised the relatives she would never steal a baby again. But of course this was a boy.

CAKE TWO IN THE UNIVERSE

IN THE MORNING HARSU WOKE ON ONE OF THE PATIOS. His heart jumped. His mother had stolen a boy. No, no, he must have dreamt it.

All the same, he made himself search the palace.

He found Daama in the kitchen, swollen with pride. The stolen boy drowsed there on a thin mattress.

"Mother, the boy's parents. They were very wrong to encourage Zamuna to boast. But they'll be desperate—" Harsu began.

"They should be thanking the stars I didn't turn them to sandstone."

She leaned near Zamuna, flicked her hand as if something opened, then brushed beside her ear as if she'd heard something. It must be a magic sign. The little boy blinked awake.

"I baked you a cake," Daama said to him. "Come."

Zamuna's eyes and handsome nostrils grew as wide as

an onager's. "Good, I'm so hungry. I had no bite of your pastries, not a nibble of my mother's barley cakes."

Daama led the boy to the reception room. Harsu followed. On a platter sat a new cake—the second cake in the universe.

Zamuna climbed on the chair and reached for the plate.

Daama laid a hand on his wrist. "I didn't say touch."

Zamuna jerked back. "B-because it's poison?"

"Handsome-but-foolish, no." She pinched his cheek and smiled. "This cake is only for looking."

Zamuna chuckled as if she must be teasing. "I'll take some home for my parents."

"Pay attention," said Daama. "Place your hands palms up, each side of the plate. Good. Now chant."

Zamuna's teeth flashed in a smile. "I am Zamuna, the most handsome …"

She laughed. "True. But that's not what I wish you to say."

"Zamuna," Harsu began, "she wants you to—"

"Don't help, Harsu. His praise must be honest. Zamuna?"

The little boy squirmed. "My powerful legs are envied by the fastest and strongest …?"

"Have you no wits? It should be obvious," said Daama. "Chant about me."

It took the whole day before Zamuna found words that made Daama smile again. If it could be called a smile when that glint was the sharp tooth of a stoat. Harsu didn't understand.

The grand-great aunt and great-great uncle were taking their time. But they would save the kid, wouldn't they?

Proud and plump, she pinched the boy's cheek again. "Go to sleep now. Woe betide you if you lose your looks."

Zamuna's eyes puddled with tears. "I want to go home."

Daama lashed out but didn't touch him. It must have been another gesture of enchantment. This time Zamuna stood like a statue, with only his eyelids flickering.

Harsu wanted to run to sleep near his father's onager. But he turned to go to his own room. He'd better stay in the palace in case the little boy needed him.

"Where are you off to? Sleep here," said Daama.

And his mother pushed the stolen boy, stiff as a carving, to Harsu's room.

Harsu lay on the mattress in the kitchen corner, his mind confused, heart jealous and sore. He'd been loyal, hadn't he? He groaned, and pulled the blanket over his head. He should call the relatives. But how? He had no idea where they were.

The door creaked. Harsu sat up.

The kitchen was silent. The bitter scent of stoat hung in the air.

Inside the door was a wet cluster of paw prints, the sign of a gleeful dancing animal. They dried even as he spotted them, the last traces the tips of claws.

He remembered more from the time when he was six. If it was like that awful time, now his mother—the werestoat—would be out for the rest of the night, dancing, triumphing, stealing eggs from the nests of songbirds.

He ran to the little bedroom and shook Zamuna.

"Get up. Run!"

Zamuna snored and mumbled.

Harsu shook him again. "Go home!"

"Cake for me," muttered Zamuna.

Harsu didn't dare try the back door, the one Daama had used. He took the boy by the shoulders and dragged him, limp and lolling, to a palace side door. Even if he had to roll the brat down the step, at least the boy would have a chance.

But when he wrestled with the lock it wouldn't open.

By now Zamuna was half awake. Harsu pulled him along by his sweaty hand. "We'll try the main door."

That didn't open either. Another side door, and another, refused to budge.

Harsu dashed to a window and searched in the gloom for a bolt to open its shutter.

"As soon as you're out you have to run," he said.

"It's too dark. I don't know the way," said Zamuna, awake properly now.

"Any way at all is better than staying here."

There was no bolt. Harsu raced to the next room and tried that shutter.

"I'm scared to go on my own. You have to come with me," Zamuna wailed.

"She's my mother. I promised to stay."

But all the ground-floor windows were fast-shuttered. And Zamuna simply refused to be pushed out of the narrow ones on the top storey. Harsu couldn't say that was a surprise.

The stolen boy sank to the floor. "My mother," he whispered. "My father."

Harsu knelt and put an arm round the little kid's skinny shoulders. His aunt had said, *All children need the comfort of a barley cake prepared by someone who loves them.*

Through the window glittered the moon.

He didn't know why he should care a jot about Zamuna. He didn't know how to make barley cakes either. Anyway, he thought they were boring.

"Come to the kitchen," said Harsu. "We've got till dawn."

The looking-cake, still untouched, sat on a kitchen table. Another table held a clutter of bowls of flour and dishes of spice. A small cauldron of bony pieces—possibly rabbit—was partly cooked. And the smallest oven rumbled.

If his mother could create in the kitchen, Harsu could too.

He pushed a chunk of firewood into the burner. Into a bowl of flour he added pepper and other spices, then stirred in water. He patted half of the dough into a circle and spread it in a shallow dish. The edge hung over the rim. He took the meat and fished out little bones. Then he cut the meat into bite-sized pieces and spooned them into the dish too.

33

Harsu patted the rest of the dough into another circle, laid it over the meat, then pinched the rims of both circles together. He slid the dish into the rumbling oven. It seemed to him that the flour should cook into a crust around what was inside.

As a half hour passed the kitchen filled with a fabulous scent.

"Your nose is like an onager's," Harsu told Zamuna. "A handsome one, naturally. Nostrils flaring and moist."

It looked as if the little boy didn't understand sarcasm.

Harsu opened the oven a crack. The top circle of dough had turned golden brown. He brought the dish out and cut into it. He'd been right. The filling was wrapped in a hot firm crust. He cut wedges that steamed, one for him, one for Zamuna.

"What's this called?" asked the boy.

"I won't bother with a name till I know it's worth it." After a while, Harsu spoke with his mouth full. "What do you think of 'snack-in-a-blanket'?"

Grinning, they ate the lot. Then Zamuna crept back to Harsu's little room.

To keep their secret, Harsu swept up every crumb.

FORGOTTEN STATUE

NEXT MORNING DAAMA WAS BACK, SMILING AND PLUMP. Not a hair of stoat, not a whiff. She looked smug, even excited.

"Harsu, there's work to do."

"Mother," Harsu began, "your relatives …"

"No boys have much of a brain. Why do you think there's work to do? I'm not going to risk all I've gained." With a human hand she patted the side of his face that had no scars. "You must agree Zamuna's mother and father are very bad parents."

Not really. "Even if they were, they are his parents," said Harsu.

"We're leaving. I am your mother so that's the end of it." She rushed off.

The bangs and crashes of packing soon clanged through the palace. "Must I do everything myself?" she cried.

Harsu ran and found her, but …

"Don't touch! You'll wreck my treasures." She dashed into her bedroom, came out tugging a sack heavy with jewels and went back for another. Then a hamper of scarves, three of headdresses, a crate of goblets from the dining hall, another heavy one that rattled with objects unknown. A pile of place mats, a bag of tiny fancy holders for salt and spices, five hundred cloaks, fifty-nine sets of cymbals. Now and then she was using charms, but even so there was much hard work and plenty of sweat.

A pile of trash grew high—a zither with broken strings, torn clothing, cracked hand-mirrors.

Before dusk her seventy carts and carriages waited, with two onagers harnessed to each. The only one she'd left in the field was Harsu's father's war-steed.

She wore a fine wool cloak and a travel headdress. It had a tiny silver carriage pinned on one side, a small silver boat on the other.

In the first cart was her throne and its cushion woven with gold. Zamuna sat next to it.

"You're taking me back to my parents, right?" He smiled at Daama.

"Give strength to my teeth and claws!" She made a flowing gesture at the boy, as if she wiped something clean.

Zamuna sat quiet now, though his eyes were a little puzzled.

Harsu busied himself with checking the harness on an

onager. *Hurry*, he thought to his relatives. *Don't you see this? Come and stop her.*

Daama glanced at the sky and hastened to climb on the hundred-and-forty-first onager. Bells chimed on its bridle.

"Harsu, bring up the rear."

He dropped back but he didn't obey. Instead he dashed to say goodbye to his father's onager. He found it waiting at the edge of the estate, near the thicket his grand-great-aunt had glanced at when she mentioned his father.

Harsu checked over his shoulder. The train of onagers had just passed out of the gate. Zamuna was craning to try to spot him.

He waved *be quiet* to the stolen boy and climbed over the fence. Then he entered the trees.

The onager leapt to come with him and nudged a pile of leaf mould. Harsu brushed it and felt hardness beneath. He eased away dirt, and there he found a man carved from sandstone. It was as tall as his father, had his father's high forehead, his strong nose, his well-shaped muscles.

Near the statue lay a warrior's arm-ring of coiled gold set with blue stones of lapis. It seemed wrong to pick it up but more wrong to leave it.

No matter how high Harsu pushed it up his arm, it was much too big. He crammed it into the pouch of his cloak with the broken pottery. It made a lump. But the cloak hid everything.

Harsu thought maybe he should say something aloud to the statue, like *Now Daama has a perfect child, she'll be a normal mother, happy and kind.*

But it would be hard to add how she'd managed to find handsome Zamuna.

He wanted to promise he would return. But he didn't know where Daama was going or what they'd do. So he just bowed to the statue. The godlet-drops burned in his heart. He knew that his father's last words to him were written on the pottery.

"Goodbye," he said. He hoped that one word in return would be enough.

PART TWO

★

THE GATE OF
TIME & PLACE

SWEET WATER

HARSU CAUGHT UP WITH THE LAST CART AT DUSK. He was pretty sure Daama hadn't noticed he'd been gone. But an angry call came from her. "You know I'm in a hurry. Where were you?"

"I had to rush to do you-know-what," he shouted back.

She snorted as if she objected.

Another *dgerr* sounded behind him. It was the war-steed, hooves shlip-shlopping on the side of the track.

He flicked his hand. "Go."

The war-steed dropped back and nibbled some grass.

By now a slender moon sailed up the sky. Harsu's pain at leaving his father's statue was still there but not so sharp.

Daama rode at greater speed, past the place where she'd stolen Zamuna. The road narrowed till a sandstone cliff rose close to the river.

"Is a boat waiting?" called Harsu. He hoped so. Then,

surely, his grand great-aunt and -uncle would notice at last. Surely they'd rescue Zamuna.

But Daaama's eyes weren't searching the river, only the cliff.

"There." She pointed to a cleft in the stone.

Her onager backed away, the harness tinkling. Daama shrieked and hauled on its reins. Bitter scent seeped around. "Harsu! Hurry up, I need some help."

Her onager gave him filthy eye-rolls. "It's not what I was expecting either," Harsu grumbled, but he managed to encourage it through the gap.

A faint glisten on the walls showed a path down to a shadowy space. The other onagers groaned and whickered while he coaxed them through. He made sure each cart had its brakes half-on so it wouldn't crash. Then he followed the onagers down to a high cavern. It was filled with the faint sound of water.

Finally, for the first time since Harsu was six, he learned something new. Over the universe was the dome of the sky. But under the plate of the universe—under the ground and the rivers, even under the salt seas—ran a vast sweet-water ocean.

The cavern roof shone with faint lights like stars. Harsu saw no humans and no animals, nor any demi-gods. Trees with silver trunks and copper leaves lined the stony underground shore. Ripples on the sweet-water sea glimmered with phosphorescence. Two tiny skiffs bobbed on the water. Another lay on the pebbles.

At the water's edge sat a building like a long box with an open archway. As Harsu neared he saw an arch at the far end as well, where the sea lapped in.

Daama rode straight for it.

"What is that?" he asked.

"Tiresome boy." Daama climbed off her onager. "It's a Ferry Gate."

"Ah. So a ferry's coming," he said.

"Ignorant as well as tiresome. I've made a difficult decision and had a long ride. I'm aching, tired out, and I still have work to do. Just hurry and do what I say."

She didn't seem so worried about the relatives now. She seemed very uncertain about something else. After taking a breath, she approached the Gate. Then she walked over the threshold. As she moved further in she touched the walls and peered up at them.

About one-third of the way along, she turned. "Zamuna, I don't want you with even a bruise if you try to run. Come in. Sit at the side out of the way. Steady yourself."

"No," he wailed. "It's the Gate of Time and Place. I don't want to be taken away. My mother told me stories …"

"Don't dare waste my strength." She made that wiping gesture at him again.

Still wailing, the boy scurried in right to the middle.

He ducked down against the wall, hands over his head.

"Harsu, lead in the cart with my throne," Daama ordered. "Then all the rest—carts and onagers."

He was certainly interested in the Gate. But clearly it terrified Zamuna.

Daama's voice echoed off the walls. "I said, hurry. Are you deaf or stupid?"

Sometimes you treat me as if I'm both, Harsu said under his breath.

He reached for the harness on a cart. But instead of sweet-talking the onager into the Gate, he loosened the straps. "Take your chance," he said. "Run."

It reared and whinnied, and the others snorted and stamped. Daama screamed at them to stop. By the time she came running, her own onager was racing off. Others were breaking their harnesses. Off they galloped through the silver trees back up the path.

Seventy carts and carriages were left. With no onagers.

Harsu made sure he didn't look directly at his mother. Her mouth opened and shut. Her shoulders slumped. In just a few moments she'd become skinny.

"I cannot and will not waste more energy. Load every cart and every carriage."

First, the cart with the throne. He took his time.

Inside, the Gate's ceiling was in shadow, too high to make out. But the walls were carved with figures of warriors, kings and gods, people with the heads of eagles or lions, even of onagers. There seemed to be writing like his father had done in tiny triangles and little sticks. There were other signs like scribbles he might make himself with his toe in the dust.

"Now take the throne off the cart. Set it down here."

As soon he'd done so, Daama sat on it without saying thank you.

Harsu trudged back for the rest of the carts, and bumped each one up into the Gate.

He'd hauled forty-five carts when he saw something move far back in the gloom where the path led down into the cavern.

A jump in his heart—the relatives at last …

But no. It was the war-steed. Foolish thing, it should have run with the others.

Harsu lost sight of it. Good. It must have gone back. All the same, he knew he'd miss it.

At last all the carriages were in the Gate. It was a huge jumble. He expected his mother would make him do it over again. But on the throne she seemed to be sleeping, or summoning energy, or just waiting with her eyes closed. At least Zamuna, still huddled against the wall, had shut up.

Harsu stood in the archway of the Ferry Gate and looked back at the cavern. He had told the relatives he was all right, but they should have come to help the stolen boy. They obviously weren't going to now. He hated them.

He checked again for the war-steed. Nothing.

This was a chance for Harsu to run too. He even rose on the balls of his feet.

But it would be wrong to leave Zamuna on his own with Daama.

Besides, hidden in the cloak, the warrior's arm-ring pressed Harsu's side. The godlet-drops fizzed in his chest.

If this was a gate that crossed time and place, how did it work?

RAIN OF MISERY

HARSU STEPPED BACK FROM THE ARCHWAY, RIGHT into the Ferry Gate. He chose the wall opposite Zamuna, hunkered down and braced himself.

At last Daama stood up from the throne. She threaded between the carts to face part of the wall. Again she ran her fingers over some of the carvings. Glints appeared, like echoes of light. She took another deep breath and began a whispering chant.

A terrible spinning began outside the Gate.

Harsu gave a gasp of excitement. The sweet-water ripples, the trees on the shore, the skiffs, the pebbled beach, the roof of the cavern became a glorious dizziness. Everything whirled except the Gate, a still point in the turning.

The spinning slowed to a rolling then a tilting—a quiver—and stopped.

Beyond the arch, sparkles on the cavern roof were further apart. The sweet-water sea splashed, then ebbed to ripples.

Harsu leapt to the near threshold. It was still on the shore. But it was a new shore, scattered with boulders. Only one rowboat floated beside a small raft. There were silver trees again but they had bare branches. Below them, drifts of leaves lay like fallen cloaks.

Harsu glanced at his mother. She was plump again.

"Where are we?" he asked.

His mother gave him a mischievous glance.

Harsu chuckled too. "Are we going up? What's it like above ground? How soon can we get there?"

"You'll see," she said.

"But how far have we come?"

Her face gleamed with pride. "Vast distances to the land of the fjords. Thousands of years."

In shock, Harsu glanced at Zamuna still huddled deep inside. His eyes were squeezed tight but he must have heard. The boy's chest heaved with a stifled sob. He'd never see his parents again.

Daama made the flowing gesture in Zamuna's direction, harder this time, as if she scrubbed at a stain. "That will deal with his memories."

Harsu hesitated. He knew what it was like to lose a parent. But maybe it was good if Zamuna forgot. They were all going to start a new life.

"This time I want only the cart with the throne," Daama said.

Harsu heaved it out of the Gate and onto the beach.

With no sign at all now that he missed his family, Zamuna climbed to his feet and strolled out too.

He seemed so smug Harsu couldn't resist teasing. "I could have used help from your huge muscles."

Zamuna's chin went up. "The most handsome boy doesn't have to work."

Harsu laughed. "If you're the most anything, I'd say the most irksome."

The little boy sniffed. "It isn't fair to use big words to me."

"No arguing." But Daama chuckled as she strode off through the grove. Zamuna scurried behind her.

A movement far back in the Ferry Gate made Harsu pause. It was his father's onager. Why had it followed him? It would serve it right if he made it help with the cart.

But a war-steed was not for this kind of work. Harsu could easily do it alone.

The path was steep, dimly lit. It was taking ages.

"Are we there yet?" Zamuna whined.

To Harsu it didn't matter. It was all an adventure.

Finally they came out on a clifftop. Below was the salt-water sea. The sun was near setting. Zamuna started to shiver. Harsu shared his cloak with him, but a cold wind wormed through the folds. A gust of rain lashed down— it rattled and stung.

Daama let out a yelp. "How extraordinary! Pellets of ice. Harsu, give me that cloak."

In its pouch lay his father's arm-ring. "No, it's far too dirty for your magnificence."

He rummaged in the cart. He found her a woollen cloak, then a blanket for Zamuna. As he tossed it over, he slipped on the ice …

Harsu steadied himself. "Look! I can slide about." He grabbed the little boy's hands and they circled, laughing.

Daama joined in, the three of them clasping hands and shouting in a cold-weather game.

"It's the best fun in my life!" Zamuna shrieked.

"Whoops," Daama cried, "keep hold of my hand."

Red-cheeked and breathless, Daama stopped at last. "We must move on before night deepens."

Yes, now a half-moon glimmered on waves that broke its reflection to fragments. Harsu tried an ice drop on his tongue. It melted at once. He set off with new energy. He'd had no idea the universe was so vast it contained a place like this, cold and bleak but so fresh and new.

The path downhill led to a settlement where lights burned through shutters.

Daama came to a halt by a house so small it could have sat on a middle-sized palace patio with space to spare.

"This will do." She squared her shoulders. "This is our new home."

SURPRISING PRAISE

HARSU WOKE ON A MATTRESS IN A ROOM WITH no window. He lay aching from yesterday's efforts. On another mattress, Zamuna blinked his eyes open. "But this isn't home."

Was he stupid? No, just young. And Daama's forgetting charm obviously wasn't as strong as the small boy's memories. Harsu sat up.

"Just don't mention your mother's barley cakes." Now he'd better go and unload the cart.

But he stepped out of the little room and found the main room already in order. His mother looked skinny again but her eyes were gleaming. She must have worked overnight. The throne commanded a corner. The oven roared.

Through a gap in the shutters it still looked cold. The icy rain had gone. Instead white flakes floated around. A few people passed on the road, greeting each other, calling and chatting. Their faces were pale, with patchy red cheeks.

Perhaps the terrible cold in this place had done it to them. The men had fur caps and wild beards, and wore leggings and boots. Their swords, if that's what they were, were not at all like his father's sickle-sword. They were long and straight.

In the new land and new time, metal could be forged strong enough for this new sort of weapon?

For the first time Harsu truly understood how many years the Ferry Gate had whirled him.

"Come, Zamuna," Daama called. "Wear your kilt, belt and headband. Sit at the table, my spicy chickpea."

Using a thick cloth she slid a cake from the oven. Then she arranged herself on the throne.

"Now, Zamuna, chant for me."

The boy gave Harsu a glance of appeal. Harsu made a face that meant *just get on with it*.

"G-generous," Zamuna began. "K-kind when your heart is—all empty—I mean gone—a hole—I mean a—an abyss."

"After all the sorrow I've suffered, you know that's not good enough," Daama said. "But try again."

"The—the universe has no better mother …" Zamuna burst into tears. "My mother made the best barley cakes ever."

Harsu grabbed the oven cloth to mop and console him.

But Daama scrubbed at Zamuna in the air again, so hard Harsu thought her fist would never unclench. This was his fault. He should never have mentioned barley cakes.

Daama crashed cauldrons around in the kitchen and prepared little pots for relish and pickles. The small storeroom had a row of shelves. On its floor stood a huge earthenware jar Harsu didn't remember ever seeing among Daama's belongings. It was empty.

She kept Zamuna dozing in the little room. But Harsu had to trek into the cold to fetch buckets of water from a pump. Again and again she sent him out to a bin of black nuggets she called *coal* for feeding the oven.

Daama muttered while she worked. Harsu realised she was rehearsing the language of this part of the fjords. Very soon he could understand a few words and speak them too. In a way he knew it was because of the godlet-drops. So he supposed being a distant relative to the Wind God had some uses.

He ducked into the little room and repeated a few of the words. "Gripe-belly," he said to Zamuna's sleepy form. "Dog-nose. But of course I would never mean you with your so-handsome snot-conk."

In a couple of days the sky was blue.

Daama appeared in clothing like the women of this country: a long tunic and too many necklaces to count at a glance. Her woven headdress was threaded with gold.

She handed Harsu stout leggings and a jacket that had a hood. Gifts from his mother.

She woke the stolen boy and bundled him into leggings too, and a jacket finer than Harsu's.

Harsu was ashamed of wishing his was the better one. After all, they were off to market. They were taking part in the life of this new world, like a normal mother with a couple of sons.

Zamuna was told to sit quietly while Harsu had to manage the cart. But he didn't mind. There was so much to look at he wished for bigger eyes. There were no onagers, just a few donkeys and even fewer horses. He thought the people they passed found his darker skin strange. They grinned at him. He grinned back.

He was sure he heard a girl giggle at his mother's gold-threaded headdress. But Daama stayed plump, confident and smiling all the way to the market square.

"Set the cart here at the edge of the throng. And both of you stay out of the way." She yanked Harsu's hood up to hide his scars.

Stalls and barrows were laden with dried meats and strings of sausages. Fish of all sizes from giant to tiddler lay with their heads on or cut off. Butter stood in creamy stacks beside towers of cheese. Bread seemed to be fat round loaves, not the flatbread Harsu was used to.

One curious customer arrived at Daama's stall, then dozens of others. The relish and pickles began selling fast.

Finally his mother took Zamuna in a gentle hand. "Come

into sight now. Pose and smile. Show everyone I am the mother to be envied above all others."

Beaming, Zamuna leapt in front of the cart, legs apart and arms akimbo.

At once an old man grumbled at him. "Dribble-beetle, dab that excuse for a chin."

For a moment Zamuna looked shocked. Then he tried a second pose, one arm at his side and his weight on one leg.

"Small-eel, out of my way," scolded a woman.

Harsu glanced at his mother. She wasn't smiling but she still looked confident.

Then a woman with a headdress like Daama's came clopping past on a horse with glittering trappings. "Little-fry's nose is up so he won't smell the poot from his own behind."

Amidst a burst of laughter from the crowd, the woman rode off.

Daama's mouth became a plum of astonishment. It shrank slowly to a prune of rage. "Home," she hissed. "Home at once."

All the way back to the cottage Zamuna wailed, "They were meant to admire me."

"It is me they should admire, you brainless nonsense," snapped Daama.

"The people here just need to get used to us—" Harsu began.

"It's not that. Don't you annoy me too. It's the fault of this so-called perfect boy!"

She bundled Zamuna inside. With a crash she opened the storeroom. With a skinny hand she slapped the huge earthenware jar.

"Cram the bumptious brat in this to consider his sins," she shouted to Harsu.

WHIRR IN THE DARK

THAT MOONLESS NIGHT, ON HIS OWN IN THE LITTLE room, Harsu's heart raced faster and faster. How could his mother do that to a child? Stuff the boy in a jar! Zamuna was certainly irritating, but he couldn't help it if he wasn't handsome to the northern people.

He heard a bang and ran to the kitchen.

A breath of wind stole through a gap between the door and the latch. Drying on the floor were the prints of a stoat, spaced to show it had raced out in such a rage that the door hadn't fastened.

Harsu crouched next to the giant container on the store-room floor. He could hardly bear to ask, "Zamuna, are you alive?"

A little snore echoed inside.

Harsu filched a dried apple and dropped it down the neck of the jar. In a moment he heard a grizzle. Thank goodness. He grabbed the rim and eased the jar onto its side.

"*Ow.* Don't bump," Zamuna moaned.

"Wake up and shut up." Harsu hauled the boy out. "Come with me."

"Don't pinch. Where are we going?"

"I can't let her treat you like this. I've no idea where to go but there must be somewhere."

They reached the open door, and the whirr of the spinning claw-top sounded in the shadows behind them.

A terrible pressure came on Harsu's muscles. He fought to grip the door frame, but the claw-top began forcing him and Zamuna back to the storeroom. He tried to brace his feet but it was impossible. He tried to dive over the claw-top but couldn't haul Zamuna with him. They fell in a heap.

The top pushed Harsu up again. He struggled against it, but it made him bundle Zamuna back into the prison-jar.

The claw-top drove Harsu on into the little room.

"Don't dare come in here," he managed to say.

At the door the claw-top prowled up and down.

Harsu collapsed on his mattress, too drained to do more than draw up his cloak. He hadn't looked perfect since he was six, and his mother had never forgiven him. Now he'd been disloyal for at least the second time. If the claw-top could tell his mother, what would she do?

In the pouch of the cloak lay the arm-ring and the broken pottery. He remembered his father speaking the words he had written. *Harsu my son the fighter. Patience is bravery.*

Wits are the best sickle-sword. What words had he added for the fourth line?

Harsu could never know because he couldn't read.

In the morning Daama didn't seem aware that Harsu and Zamuna had tried to escape. But Harsu saw an apple core next to the prison-jar. Before she noticed it he kicked it outside.

"Don't think you can play," she snapped. "Bring in that sack. Peel the onions."

The sack was as big as Zamuna. Peeling so many onions made Harsu's nose clog. When he had to go the storeroom, he bumped the earthenware jar. "Oh, sorry." He bumped it again and gave it a bash.

After five hundred onions it was afternoon. After two hundred more—

"Harsu," Daama said. "Bring the basket." It held tiny cakes that smelled of almonds.

The godlet-drops ran through Harsu, cold as ice.

"Only one basket? That must be for a very small market," he said, unsmiling. "Is it worth the bother?"

"None of your cheek," she hissed. "First, the brat's looks mean nothing to the savages who are so stupid they live in this cold land. Second, his praise has become too feeble to please me. Third, he grizzles. I deserve a perfect child."

A BRUISE & A WETTING

DAAMA STRODE AHEAD FAR FROM THE VILLAGE. Harsu wanted to heave the basket into the under-growth, into a stream or over a cliff, but what good would that do? He cursed the claw-top. He cursed under his breath at a grand-great-aunt who hadn't come. He cursed at a great-great-uncle who hadn't noticed how Daama had twisted her promise. He cursed demi-gods and other rela-tives of whatever kind who were too weak to travel through space and time.

Finally she stopped at a bay with a stony beach. A long-boat sat on the calm water of the fjord.

Harsu's mother sniffed the air. Then she waved at the water with a peculiar smoothing gesture. Wind started to chop at the sea in the fjord but the bay stayed flat as a mirror.

She grabbed the basket and shoved Harsu behind bushes of thorns.

"Why always thorns?" he complained.

But she'd vanished from view.

The longboat turned and headed towards them. Soon Harsu could make out ten sets of oars, two rowers to each, men and women with their hair tied in warrior-knots.

At the stern stood a strong pair with a boy between them. He seemed nearly Harsu's age and had curly fair hair. He looked lively—possibly perfect.

But Harsu relaxed. Surely this boy was too old to please Daama. Besides, the parents wouldn't leave him alone on the beach, and there were twenty other grown-ups.

Laughing, the rowers dipped the oars to keep the boat in one spot.

"Up!" shouted the warrior father.

The rowers lifted the oars out of the water and held them parallel above the sea. The man jumped and balanced on the railing. The woman threw him two swords one after the other. He held them high.

"Steady!" He studied the slight movement of the longboat. Then he sprang on the rearmost oar. At once he leapt to the next and the next, each time throwing a sword up and catching it. On he leapt to the fourth and fifth …

"Pedar Ragnason, oar-leaper," the woman cried.

"Sword-juggler!" yelled the boy.

Sixth, seventh—the man reached the tenth and last oar.

Swords in one hand, he swung under the prow, up on the other side, and was oar-leaping again—fourteen—fifteen …

At the eighteenth oar, the warrior wavered at last.

He managed to fling the swords and himself into the boat, then sprang up grinning.

"Foot-stumbler!" shouted the woman.

A rower snatched up a cow-horn flute and played a mocking blast.

Harsu covered his own ripple of laughter. The warrior mother would be such fun. How he wished he still had his own father. If it weren't for Zamuna, Harsu would swim out to them, scramble in and sail off.

The boy jumped up and down. "My turn! I'll show you, Modir."

Every warrior laughed.

The warrior mother tried to ruffle his hair but the boy dodged. "You'd show me nothing, Ragnar," she said. "I've run the oars myself, and better than your fadir."

The man saluted her, fist to his heart. "She's right, Ragnar little-pup. Practise at home in the yard first."

"But Fadir!" shouted the boy.

"Wait."

The parents and warriors ignored the boy while the oars were adjusted up and down again. Harsu guessed they were figuring the best angle to help the next runner.

Ragnar bounced on his toes. He glanced at his parents, took a step back, then sprang on the railing. "Oar-flier!" he yelled.

"Stop!" the father roared.

But the boy leapt on the first oar, then the next. Harsu nearly cheered. Ragnar teetered, yelled and leapt again. But he missed his footing.

He dropped into the sea.

The father dived after him. A rower helped lift the boy out by the scruff of his neck. For a moment Ragnar lay still.

Harsu went sweaty with relief when the boy rolled on his side, then struggled up.

The warrior mother stood, her face like a thundercloud. The father looked as grim as thunder itself.

Not a word was said. But the rowers turned the boat so the prow crunched into the pebbles. Ragnar climbed down by himself. Nobody went with him.

The father's voice rang out at last. "The first rule of my longboat is to obey me. Learn it now."

The mother wrapped a bundle of clothing, thrust the cow-horn flute into it and cast it all onto the beach. "Dry clothes. Only because the night will be cold and I am your modir. Play the flute if you're scared of demons. It will chase them away."

Harsu crouched where he was, head full of thoughts more painful than thorns.

The mother's back stayed as straight as a queen's. The father stood straight as a king while the longboat sailed away over the fjord.

Alone on the beach, Ragnar shrugged. He unwrapped the bundle but didn't bother with dry clothes, just dragged a cloak round himself and lay down with the rest as a pillow. He waggled a foot in the air and played farts on the flute.

Daama appeared with the basket. Her necklaces rattled. Ragnar eyed her, then turned away.

Harsu opened his mouth to yell, *She's a werestoat*, but his throat was bound tight.

"Brave-child, handsome-strong-boy, too old to grizzle," Daama said in a voice sweet as honey. "Yet you are hurt."

Ragnar shrugged. "To a son of the fjords, a bruise and a wetting are a sneeze and a tickle."

"Risk-taker." Her teeth gleamed.

Ragnar shrugged again. "If I am to go a-viking, my parents say I have to take risks."

"But you took a risk and they deserted you," Daama replied.

He jumped up and grinned. "I'm punished for not obeying. I expected it. It's hardly the first time. They'll be back tomorrow."

Daama smiled. "Here at last is a child who will never weaken."

"And I'll be a man who never weakens." Ragnar blasted the flute.

Daama's smile stayed steady but her eyes narrowed. "Your

parents deserted you," she repeated. "They are very bad parents. You will be eager to obey a good mother."

The boy snorted.

She held out the basket. Harsu managed a strangled cry.

Ragnar stuck his chin in the air. "Going hungry is part of the punishment."

But then, with a shout of laughter, he snatched a pastry.

FIRST PIES IN THE UNIVERSE

T HE NEW STOLEN BOY SNORED IN THE KITCHEN CORNER, the cow-horn flute still in his hand.

Plump as a cake, Daama shut the oven door. "Harsu, what a sour face. Wash the pots while I find a warm snack." Almost dancing, she slipped outside.

Sour! She'd stolen another boy. He felt worse than sour.

What was the use of his being patient since he was six? And why in the universe did his mother dirty so many dishes and cauldrons for a cake she refused to let anyone eat? Surely she could find an enchantment to wash the pots.

Harsu filled a bucket from the pump and poured some in a basin. While he splashed suds and dirty water, he made whatever parts of her magic signs he could remember. She wouldn't teach him. All right, he'd learn for himself.

At last he crashed a clean cauldron up on its hook. The boy gave a groan. Harsu swung around.

Ragnar scrambled up on one knee. "Where's that woman?

Is this her house? Mmm, I smell baking again." He pointed with the flute. "A lordly chair. Where did she steal it?" He jumped on the seat of the throne, set a foot on its back and leapt off before it toppled.

"Food!" He headed for the storeroom.

"Stop," said Harsu, "listen to me …"

Ragnar was already staring down the neck of the giant container. "A boy? Ha!" He stuck his head in. "Greetings, snoring-dolt!"

Harsu grabbed him. "You were snoring too. Don't upset him. For your own sake, lie back on the mattress."

A grizzle echoed inside the prison-jar.

Harsu tried his mother's calming sign to quiet Zamuna. But the outer door started to open, so he turned the smoothing into a scratch of his ear. Then he plunged his hands back in the dishwater.

Ragnar flung himself down with his eyes shut—no, there was a glint.

Wiping small feathers off her lips, Daama glanced around the kitchen. Then she drew a huge round cake out of the oven. She eased it onto a platter, spread it with a paste of ground almonds and began to decorate it with a circle of walnuts.

"This new child is the one," she crooned to herself. "He's still young enough. He's blemish-free. He's bursting with courage."

A claw of jealousy scratched Harsu's heart again. "Ragnar will grow," he said. "Just as I will, any day."

Daama glanced at him and dusted her hands. She glided to a cupboard and fetched a small container. "I certainly don't want him any older."

She bent over Ragnar, eyes shut on the mattress. "Open wide." In a swift motion she slid something into his mouth.

Ragnar tried to spit but couldn't. *"Ach!* What a taste."

Harsu had seen that container before. The black pellet that tasted of pitch. What a fool beyond fools—he realised only now it had stopped him growing. His hand went to his chin. No hair, not even fluff. *Every boy creates a quagmire of bedevilment*, she'd said. Yet she couldn't bear the idea of him becoming a man.

Fury rose in him. But in his chest the godlet-drops stirred as if they said *wait*, just as his warrior father had said when he wrote those words about patience.

But I have waited, Harsu cried inside. *I will not wait forever*.

"Now up," Daama said to Ragnar. "Sit on that chair."

"When I'm ready," said Ragnar.

Daama made the calming sign, like smoothing, like drawing a curtain. Harsu watched closely—yes, he'd had the sign right.

But how exactly did she do the wake sign? He turned towards the storeroom so she couldn't see him try: his fingers *flicked* like an eye opening, *brushed* beside his ear. Zamuna's prison-jar rocked a little.

"Ragnar, you will sit," said Daama.

"Sitting's for weaklings. I'm off home." Ragnar made for the door.

She repeated the smoothing sign, harder.

Ragnar wavered. He blinked. Then he shrugged and turned back to the room.

Daama placed the cake on the table, near the gold server and the knife with the lapis hilt. "Sit," she said again.

The northern boy made a grab for the knife.

"No touching! Hear these rules." Daama softened her voice. "First, you need to know I am the daughter of the Wind God."

Ragnar laughed. "Njord? He has no children. And his wife chose him by accident. *Phht!* Was she furious."

Daama's eyes flew wide with surprise.

Ragnar grinned. "I knew you were foreign."

Her face tightened. "The Wind God has thousands of children who roam over the plate of the universe and through the dome of the sky."

The boy laughed again. "The universe is not a plate. It has seven realms carried in the branches of the great ash tree. I had that all beaten into me, so my parents thought. Some of it stuck." He jumped from the chair and headed for the throne again.

Daama seized him. "Behave. I am generous. There's no better mother in any universe. Sit. Palms up. You will give me praise."

Ragnar blew a rude noise. But he sat and thumped grubby hands each side of the plate. "If you like. Praise? Cake-cooker … cake-mixer … I know. Thief of the lordly chair."

"Don't dare call me a thief," Daama said. "The throne is mine."

The prison-jar rocked again and Zamuna's shiny black hair appeared. He squinted at Ragnar. "Another boy?"

"How did he wake?" Daama cried.

Harsu's fingers tingled—it must have been the sign he had tried.

"But his hair's like fleece from a sheep. He's ugly," Zamuna complained. "And he's got a cake. That's not fair. Only the most handsome shall have a cake."

"You are definitely the most stupid," muttered Harsu.

"If I need your opinion, I'll ask for it," his mother told him.

"Yes, you shut up," shouted Zamuna. "You can't say I'm stupid. I am good-looking."

Ragnar hooted. "No wonder you store that dolt in a pickle jar."

Zamuna ducked down, came up with a piece of apple and chucked it at Ragnar. It hit Daama instead.

The brat's handsome chin dropped with fright. "It's Harsu's fault! He keeps giving me apples."

Daama turned an angry look on Harsu.

"He baked a snack too." Zamuna ducked down again.

Daama scratched a furious enchantment over the mouth of the prison-jar.

Ragnar's face showed he understood at last that he was in danger. "She's a demon!" He sprang for the outside door.

She drew a sign as fierce as the slicing of a sickle-sword. The boy buckled at the knees and fell flat on his face.

Bristles began sprouting under Daama's chin. "Harsu, you baked something in my kitchen. When?"

Harsu thought fast. "I was ashamed to tell you. I over-reached myself. My humble creation could never match your remarkable invention of the first cake in the universe."

"Match mine?" Her arm rose—he saw the hints of claws. "Match mine!"

Then all of a sudden she pealed with laughter. "Match my invention!" The claws vanished. So did the bristles.

Finally Daama wiped her eyes. "As if your creation could ever match mine. You should be ashamed for even trying. But it does suggest surprising enterprise. Show me at once."

HALF-TROLL SNOT

I T TOOK ALL DAY FOR HARSU TO SHOW DAAMA HOW TO make snack-in-a-blanket. She kept Zamuna snoring in the jar, Ragnar on the mattress.

Her first try burned black on top. She tried a smaller snack-in-a-blanket, then one even smaller. He lost count of how many times he refilled the coal bucket. Finally she set six little round ones and six little square ones on a tray. When she pulled it from the oven the steam was so delicious that Harsu could taste it.

She spun about. "My talent's remarkable. Now I need a name for my little brain-children."

"I told you I called mine snack-in-a-blanket," Harsu said. "These ones are even more snack-like."

She ignored him. With a fingernail, she scratched triangles and lines in a drift of flour on the kitchen table, smoothed them out and scratched something new.

"Don't stare. You've seen people writing." She gazed at it

herself. "Ah. Pies, that's the name. Pies. No one else in all the universe has used the word yet."

Harsu's name for them was better. Sadly, it was not worth saying so.

Though Daama was happy now, she didn't let Zamuna out of the prison-jar. By next market-day morning, he still snored there. She scrubbed the forgetting sign, smoothed the be-calm sign, and set the claw-top spinning to keep Ragnar drowsing on his mattress.

"My patience with this new boy surprises even me," she told Harsu. "But it's not logical to take him with us till he can behave. It's obvious that these people of the fjords will take a while to appreciate what I am. Fill the cart with my pies. Stack them carefully. They'll bring me praise on which I shall build. I said be careful. And hurry up."

Harsu could hardly believe how fast the snacks-in-blankets— he meant pies—started to sell. It was obvious to him they'd been invented again in the thousands of years since he did it. He caught similar scents from parcels in the arms of some of the crowd. But perhaps they weren't actually called pies. And Daama's did seem especially popular.

She called him to stand next to her and help. He wrapped parcel after parcel. Children hung about, drooling. Their parents crowded around too, wrapped in fur coats and hats.

"Second-rate pelts from mangy animals," Daama muttered. But her eyes twinkled. Her cheeks were rounder and rosier. Not a trace of down showed under her chin.

The horseback lady clopped up again. "I see no skinny braggart with you today, good woman," she cried as she passed.

Daama gave a thin smile. "I am far finer than her. Soon she'll know it."

In a few moments a stout couple shoved in front of everyone else. "We'll take the last of these."

Daama pushed Harsu aside and wrapped the pies with her own hands. She put on a sorrowful smile. "All my babies," she said on a dying note. "My beautiful babies, gone, every one. My heart is bereft."

"Ach, such moaning," the woman said. "Any mother's heart knows terrible pain." The couple strode away with the parcel of pies.

In front of Harsu's eyes Daama grew skinny. "As if the great-granddaughter of the Wind God is *any mother*. I am the mother to end all, and I will prove it."

Back in the little house Daama hurled herself around the kitchen mixing a looking-cake and slammed it into the oven. The middle was still soggy when she hauled it out again with skinny hands. She banged it on the table, woke Ragnar with a *flick* and a *brush*, and dragged him to the chair.

"Praise me at once."

He shrugged. "*Phtt.* Batter-stirrer, smell-producer."

Daama gave a shriek of rage. She beat him with the gold server and threw it aside. She grabbed the knife of celebration and thumped him with the hilt again and again.

He only roared with laughter, side-stepped and made crazy faces. At last she cast a sign that hurled him back onto his mattress.

The cry of the werestoat came from her throat. The backs of her hands darkened with fur. It appeared on her cheeks. She shrank to stoat size and stormed from the house with a scrabble of claws.

Harsu's heart raced. He fetched a dab of butter to soothe Ragnar's bruises. "Don't keep maddening her."

Ragnar's eyes opened, and he sneezed. "Look, fur's floating in the space she left. She's been shedding."

"Everything is a joke to you. You're older than Zamuna, be more sensible. All we have to do is keep her happy. Then somehow I'll get you away."

Ragnar sat up. "I hear you. But I'm a fighter, the son of warriors."

"My father was a warrior too," Harsu replied. "And a physician. He told me to be patient."

"So where is he now?" Ragnar asked.

Harsu thought of the sandstone statue, the drift of leaf mould. He had to clear his throat before he spoke. "He also said wits are the best sickle-sword. He wrote the signs for me and I still have them."

Ragnar grinned. "My mother told me wits are the best weapon. All parents must tell their children the same so-called wisdom." He rolled to Zamuna's jar and gave it a kick. "Hey, smug-bum, silly-down-duckie. I am Risk-taker."

The prison-jar rocked.

Ragnar kicked it again. "Pretty-boy. Skinny thin-pins."

Harsu tried to make the calming sign but Ragnar whacked his hand and by accident his fingers flicked to make half the sign for *wake*.

The boy dodged to a corner and snatched something up. "Dead mouse!" He pitched it into the prison-jar.

Zamuna shrieked. The jar tipped, and out he scrambled. He seized Ragnar's throat. "Half-troll snot!"

Ragnar choked but only with laughter. "Stink-piglet!"

Harsu tried to pull them apart. They both fell on him, kicking, shout-laughing, play-punching and yelling. He couldn't help laughing too and punched back, the three of them wrestling all over the floor …

The outer door flung wide. Daama stood there, human size but still part-stoat.

Her stoat nose twitched. With stoat claws she pulled the spinning top from her apron and sent it whirling. Zamuna dropped asleep with a last grizzle. Ragnar, too, with a final snort.

"The new boy's even worse than the first," she hissed. "The hooligan goes into a container this very minute."

"He belongs with his parents," said Harsu. "Give him back."

Daama's head snapped round. Something glinted on her muzzle. She brushed it, and a flake of eggshell fell to the floor. "What's mine stays mine always."

"There's no other jar big enough—" Harsu began.

With a thump a new container appeared next to Zamuna's.

"Bundle the lout into it. Then you'll pack the cart."

"But market's over …"

"Market! Do you think the favourite daughter of a daughter of a daughter of the Wind God is an idiot? Why in the universe should I stay in this place where insolent women on horseback pour scorn on me? I will find another place where people admire me as I deserve."

THE WORD CANNOT

THE GODLET-DROPS GAVE HARSU STRENGTH AS HE lifted Ragnar's prison-jar into the cart. He rapped it hard.

"Don't you dare wake him," Daama snapped.

"Just checking," said Harsu.

Her thin fingers signed the sleep charm. Then she disappeared into the house for more baggage.

"Ragnar. Wake." Harsu tried the *flick* and *brush* of the wake sign and hit the jar again. "It's your last chance to go home."

"Waiting my chance," mumbled Ragnar.

"The chance is now!"

But Daama's sleep charm was fresh and strong. Ragnar gave a drowsy chuckle. "You and me, adventures. Leave smugworm, pretty-chin behind ..."

The chuckle turned into a snore. But Harsu felt a warmth that meant, even though Ragnar enraged him, he had a friend.

Daama emerged with the last load. Two prison-jars made the cart much heavier now. The throne itself had been heavy enough. The wheels refused to roll. Harsu tried again.

"Hopeless boy, be careful of my belongings," Daama cried.

Hauling and shoving, Harsu managed the cart to the clifftop, then eased it down the underground track to the sparkling cavern and silver grove. The rowboat lay drawn up on the pebbles but the raft had gone.

The Ferry Gate was just as before, with Daama's other carts and belongings still inside. She rushed to inspect them.

Harsu's father's onager lifted its head from nibbling silver grass. *Dgerr.*

It eyed Daama but she still hadn't noticed it. Behind her back it shlip-shlopped through the arch into the Gate and nosed around the walls. Then it settled out of sight.

Finally Harsu had the cart and prison-jars into the Ferry Gate.

"How will you know where to go?" he asked Daama.

"I've learned exactly how to guide the Gate," she replied.

She was certainly powerful but—really?

"It would be easiest to go back," said Harsu. "Home, to the palace."

His mother fixed him with a look that chilled him through. "The Gate goes only one way. The way I tell it."

She seemed plumper again as she turned to examine the walls. This time she stepped further in.

Harsu watched every movement. Once again her finger-tips skimmed most of the carvings but lingered on others. He recognised now that she took note of the signs like those his father had used. Other signs were like markings he'd seen on some stalls at the northern market. Again something glinted now and then. He listened to the chant she whispered, about eyes and time, heart and place.

At last she stepped back to the throne. Her eyes closed.

Harsu sat with his back against a crate. He settled his cloak so the copper tokens didn't chime and his father's arm-ring and the pieces of pottery didn't dig into him. He should examine the pottery lentil—it might help him learn to read.

The godlet-drops answered the thought with a warming glow.

Then the whirling began. The sparkles on the roof of the cavern, the sweet-water sea, everything outside the Gate became lines of light, then a dizzying tangle …

… till the spinning slowed.

Outside the Ferry Gate lay a new cavern. Roof and sea sparkled and glimmered.

His mother nudged him with her foot. She was as plump as ever he'd seen. She wore a black dress and long white apron. A white bonnet was tied in a bow under her chin. Her clothes had never been so plain.

"What are you staring at?" she asked.

"You look … refined," he said.

He heard *dgerr* from the war-steed in the shadows.

She frowned.

"Elegant," Harsu hurried to add in case she noticed the onager. "Sleek like a bird."

"A bird," she said. "Eggs. I'll need eggs fast." She tossed him a bundle of cloth. "Change into these, quick."

He unfolded a pair of baggy brown leggings and scrambled into them. They reached just below his knees.

"They're breeches. It is the fashion here." Neat human teeth showed in her smile. "Your old boots are still nice and stout. Your shirt and jacket are perfectly fine."

He didn't much like the breeches but they were another gift. And the plain dress she wore must mean she was definitely better prepared for this place than she'd been for the land of the north. He began to feel hopeful.

Ragnar would just have to settle down. The Ferry Gate didn't go back in time, Daama had said. Once they'd found another home, once they were comfortable, Harsu would be able to figure out how she worked her enchantments. He'd find a way to make himself and Ragnar grow as they should.

Daama left the throne in the Gate but made Harsu load one of the crates from another cart. It was heavy and not well packed. Inside it, things slid around.

When at last he pushed the cart out of the Gate, four little boats were bobbing on the ripples. There were taller trees in the grove, branches rustling with copper leaves.

He sweated after his mother through the cavern and up a path to this new part of the world. It still looked like a plate to him: streams laced through spreading marshes. The sky looked like a dome where clouds floated and billowed.

"This is England," Daama said. "It has much better weather than the icy north. No hooligans to give boys a bad example. Come."

Harsu put his shoulder to the back of the cart but the wheels stuck in the boggy ground.

"I can't budge this weight," he groaned. "Why don't you use magic or—"

She flung up her hands. "The ears of she who is descended from the Wind God cannot hear the word *can't*. I've given you clothing. I'm leading the way. Are you incompetent?"

"Of course not." Words flew out of him. "I'm the son of a daughter of a daughter of one of the Wind God's who-cares-how-many thousands of children."

"I should never expect a child to understand how difficult it is to be a mother." Daama marched fast for a few moments, then started to puff.

Harsu bit his lips together hard. He didn't want the burden of her on the cart too.

—

82

Hours later they found a village and an empty cottage. Daama strode in and was soon out again.

"I show such courage. This hovel could have sat in the palace broom closet with space to spare. There's only one small bedroom and it's mine. There's a cranny I can call a pantry. Harsu, sleep on the kitchen floor. First, get that crate to my room. If you break what's in it, you're in trouble."

"I need a moment." Harsu leaned over, hands on his knees.

"I'm weary too," his mother said. "Do you hear me complaining?"

He lifted the crate and managed three steps. Then it slipped. A corner crunched on the ground.

Inside was an unmistakable sound. Broken pottery.

For a breath, his mother didn't move. Then she made a fierce sign at the crate and it disappeared.

"Now the jars," she snapped, and darted inside. She must have charmed the crate to her room.

Why couldn't she just charm everything into place? Harsu shook a fist. Then he rolled Zamuna's jar over the threshold. *"Ow,"* came from inside.

He set it upright in the pantry nook and went back for Ragnar's. It banged when he set it against the wall.

"Smoke and fire, am I going to bash you," Ragnar groaned.

"Be glad you're alive," Harsu muttered.

"I am not glad!"

"That's because you're ugly," cried Zamuna.

"You shut up," said Harsu.

"You can't tell a handsome boy what to do," Zamuna complained.

"Zamuna, scrawny-worm," Ragnar started to sing. *"Feeble fart-squeal."*

Zamuna's scream of rage echoed higher and higher.

"Quiet!" Daama stood in her doorway. Her clothes were looser. Her shoulders had hunched. She flung the claw-top. It hummed around the jars, and the boys fell silent as if they'd choked.

Her voice thrummed with rage. "I have wasted far too much of my precious energy. My remarkable patience has drained completely."

For a moment Harsu hoped she'd finished.

She hadn't. "These boys have proven they are impossible. I cannot show either of these little monsters, these thugs, in this respectable place. I have no option. I'm getting a girl."

MUSKET & GLOOM

SHOCK WHIRLED AROUND HARSU. GETTING A GIRL! Daama was supposed to settle down in the new country. Then his hand flew up to hide a grin. His grand-great-aunt had said Daama was a horror when she was young. If Daama thought a girl would be more biddable than boys, she might get a shock of her own.

Even so, the minute his mother left the cottage again, Harsu signed the wake charm over Ragnar's prison-jar. He bashed it as well.

"Did you hear what she said? She'll catch a girl."

A sleepy groan. "So?"

"So it's terrible."

"No worse than kidnapping me and pretty-worm. A girl can stick up for herself. Girls fight. Your mother must have been a girl once and look at her now."

"Ragnar, you're as useless as little pretty-boy. You just let her send you to sleep."

Ragnar yawned long and loud. "The right moment will come for me to escape. I'm hoarding my strength and my wits."

"You can't hoard wits if you don't have any. Listen, before she stole Zamuna she stole two babies, then some twins. My relatives saved them, but they can't or won't come to save anyone else. What I'm trying to get through your thick head is, my mother plans to steal another child."

He heard struggling inside the jar. Ragnar's fair curls rose into view and he peered over the rim.

"Why steal anyone? She has a son and you're trouble enough."

Harsu showed Ragnar his fist. "I'll give you trouble. Look at my face."

Ragnar squinted. "Mottles and scars. But not burn or battle scars. I guess smallpox."

"That's why she steals," said Harsu. "I'm not perfect. I'm not handsome."

Ragnar shrugged. "You probably never were."

Harsu's fist clenched tighter. "I'm not perfect because my father didn't stop me from being scarred."

"Huh?" said Ragnar.

"My father," Harsu repeated. "He was a warrior and a physician, and …"

"You said that before. So what? Life's what you make it." Ragnar slumped back into the jar and snored again.

It was no use trying to get help or sense out of Zamuna. Harsu sagged down in a corner.

After a moment he reached into the pouch of the cloak, pulled out the pieces of pottery lentil and fitted them together again. On the side with his father's writing, the sticks and triangles still made no sense. Then something seemed to happen in his eyes and brain. He managed to read: *Harsu my son the fighter/patience is bravery/wits are the best sickle-sword.* His father had said the fourth and last line when Harsu was in a fever-dream. He couldn't actually figure the signs out but he could remember now, his father saying: *time and stone peel away.*

He turned the lentil to the student's side. In his own childish marks he saw: *Harsu my son.*

Daama spent days gathering English herbs, pottering about the small kitchen. If she'd meant what she'd said about catching a girl, she might have forgotten. The stolen boys breathed on, snoring, in the prison-jars.

Harsu drew water from a well in an old bucket. He chopped onions and rolled out pastry. He eyed the lines and triangles Daama drew with a fingertip in flour drifts while she baked.

Daama began to use a feather—a quill—she dipped into black liquid called ink, and scribbled away making curly marks on some parchment as well. It kept rolling up as she worked. The only way Harsu could see clearly was over her shoulder.

"What's the matter with you?" his mother asked.

It felt foolish to admit he was trying to read what he thought might be English words. "Onion juice makes me squint," he said.

He watched the road outside. There were many more horses and dozens of carriages. Some had four horses and raced along. Was it safe for a human body to jolt about like that? Were the English different in that way? Mind you, Harsu guessed, in its own way the Ferry Gate went pretty fast and certainly far.

Many of the passers-by had pale faces like the northern folk. Everyone seemed especially glum. Their black clothes were neat and clean. Some men had long swords. Others had things slung on straps over their shoulders or on their belts. What could they be?

Again his mother didn't teach him the new language. Just as it had happened in the north, Harsu began to understand it and use it anyway.

And he figured that if Daama finally let the boys out, they'd need the language too. So he whispered word-hints and other bits and pieces into the silent jars.

"There isn't a king. The ruler is called the Lord Protector. On their belts men carry strange things—weapons called pistols. I saw one with a bigger pistol-weapon but he called it a musket. On days called Sunday, most people stay indoors once they've visited church. I think it must be like a temple. Ragnar, do you know what a temple ... Oh, never mind. It's to do with prayers and stuff. I'm pretty sure the English church has nothing to do with any Wind God. I don't have a clue what they believe about the universe ..."

Only snoring came from the prison-jars.

Daama went to market at last. As soon as customers bought her pies, they hid them as if any treats had to be smuggled.

A few of the other stalls had placards above them with the curly writing. Harsu figured out some words from the goods being sold. He tried copying them with a stick scratching in dirt. *Meate. Fine hattes. Cures for all ylls.* But he wasn't sure what it all meant.

At the end of these first weeks his mother was even-tempered, neither skinny nor plump. A girl hadn't been mentioned again. Harsu was pretty sure she'd decided it was enough to have three boys. In time she would learn how to manage them.

POPPET & PASTRY

L ATE ONE AFTERNOON DAAMA HUMMED A TUNE FROM long ago. *"Sweet bee has a sting..."* Harsu started to join in. Then his heart started to thud. His mother was packing pastries into a basket.

Over the two prison-jars Daama drew the calming charm. She set the claw-top spinning around the jars as well.

"Bring the basket," she told Harsu.

What had Ragnar said? It had been close enough to what his father meant: hoard your strength and wits till the right time. Somehow Harsu had to stop her from stealing another child, boy or girl.

The round white cap hid Daama's long black hair. Her plain white apron reached almost to the ground. She headed to the edge of the forest. Leaves shimmered in late sun. Close by lay a fine manor house with two storeys, windows of glass that glinted, and many chimneys. It was as big as her old palace near the river bank where she'd stolen Zamuna.

A side door opened. Out slipped a small figure, bundled in a cloak with a hood. It hurried into the woods.

His mother beckoned Harsu to stay close while she slunk along.

The figure seemed to check no one was watching. A pale hand pushed the hood back, unfastened the cloak and let it fall.

It was a girl maybe eight years old. She held a long-handled racket. A blue ribbon tied back her red curls. Her dress had puffed sleeves and a wide lace collar, a sash tied with a bow. The skirt was a blue so bright it made Harsu blink.

The little redhead stood as if she were speaking to a great audience. "Oliver Cromwell, Lord Protector of England! You killed the King. Even in their own house my timid guardians dare not defy you. *Pish* to you, Lord Protector. I will break every one of your rules this very day."

Harsu surprised himself with a huff of a laugh. Ragnar would like her. Zamuna—probably not. Anyway, Harsu was here to make sure they never even met her.

"Rule One, do not go walking on a Sunday." The girl put her nose in the air. "See, I have walked by myself into the woods. Two, do not wear a garment in any bright hue. My blue satin had been on me only twice before you killed the King." Scowling, she tugged at her waist under the sash. "Now it is almost tight and I am not permitted to have a new one. Rule Three, do not dance. Ha!" She pointed her little shoes back and forth and twirled about. "Four, play no sport." She brandished the racket.

Daama whisked past Harsu, grabbed the basket from him and was hidden again.

"Five! Do not swear." The little girl dropped the racket and pulled a roll of paper out of a pocket-pouch tied at her waist. "I have written down many swear words that my uncle says when he thinks my sister and I do not hear him." She gave a giggle. "Six, do not sing." She fetched a little doll out of the pocket. It looked made of straw. "And you do not like toys, but here is my favourite poppet. Now, watch me break three rules together."

While she danced with her doll she sang, high and sweet. *"Beshrew thee, Oliver Cromwell, Lord Protector. Thou art a warty runagate toad."*

Harsu covered his mouth to stop snorting like an onager.

Still singing, the girl danced further into the woods. Daama's pale apron moved nearby.

Harsu waited for his moment.

In the distance came the drumming of hoof-beats. The girl startled. She ran and pressed herself against the trunk of an elm. The blue dress and its white collar gleamed in the shadow. Even her red hair gave her away. It might be her guardian coming to find her. It could be one of Cromwell's soldiers who would punish her and her family. But Harsu's mother was worse than anything.

The horse and rider came hurtling through the trees.

Harsu sprang right in front of them. "Stop!"

The horse whinnied and reared. Its hooves nearly struck Harsu but the man reined it in. "What's this? Who are you? Have you seen my niece?"

"Help!" shouted Harsu.

The air hummed like night wasps starting to swarm. Daama moved into view. With a smile, she held up the basket. "Take, eat," she said to the rider.

The man gave a slow shake of his head as if in a dream. "My niece …" he said again.

"Eat," Daama repeated.

His hand went out—he chose a pastry—he bit into it.

Daama held a pastry out for the horse too. It shied away, neighing. Then off it galloped with the girl's uncle flopping, drowsing, over its neck.

The forest was silent.

"I hardly needed you to help. But well done," Daama said softly to Harsu.

What? In front of his eyes she was fattening, pleased with him.

The girl took a step.

"Child," Daama purred. "I hope you are not harmed."

The girl let out a laugh. "You sound just like my nurse. You're as fat as her too. I call her my dough-nurse, made of lumps ready for kneading."

A whiff of stoat floated about, but Daama purred on. "A girl as rosy as you, with such spirit, always deserves to wear the brightest gown. What is your name?"

"Blanche." The girl pushed the poppet back into her pocket. "My uncle will likely beat me with a birch rod. But I must go home now."

"A child with hair as rich as yours should belong to the gentlest of guardians," Daama said. "I am awash in an ocean of tears, for I have no children. You are my new comfort."

"I think not," said Blanche. "I shall run home. To suffer the rod will be horrid but very soon over. My aunt will weep and weep, and afterwards my sister will steal in to me with a spoon of sugar."

"Sweet sugar would break another rule of the Protector." Daama lifted the basket. "A nibble of these would break the rule now. How many is that?"

Before Harsu could call *stop* again, Blanche thrust her hand into the basket, pulled out a tart and took a bite.

"Seven," she cried, "and each rule more foolish than the one before."

DOUGH-LADY

THE SUN HAD SET. BACK IN THE HOVEL, BLANCHE SLEPT on the mattress. Daama fetched a bowl of raw eggs and collapsed in a chair.

Harsu couldn't bear to see her crunching into them. He curled up in the old cloak and fingered the signs etched into the discs. What would his father do? How would his father find the right moment to free the girl—to free all the stolen children? His mind was so crammed with questions that he knew he'd never sleep.

But he sat up to early sunshine. Daama was signing *wake* with wide gestures beside Blanche's mattress.

The girl's eyes fluttered open. "What is this place? Where is my dough-nurse? I want my aunt. I want my sister."

With a smaller movement, Daama signed the forgetting charm.

After a second or two Blanche began poking about.

Harsu expected Daama to stop her. His mother just

seemed amused and went to scribble with more ink on another parchment.

Blanche pulled at the curtain over the pantry nook. "I am famished. Can anything be here to break my fast? Verily, jars of such size! What can be in them?" She danced around, found a stool to climb on and teetered as she stuck her nose in Zamuna's jar. "What a jape! A boy. How cross he looks. What a smell he makes. *Pish!*"

She clattered the stool against the second jar. "Another boy? *Pish* to you too. How rough you look."

Ragnar's hands appeared, then his head and an elbow. The jar overbalanced. Daama signed the calming charm, and he lay half-out on the floor, asleep.

Blanche giggled, ran to the door and rattled the knob. "Dough-lady, prithee, open. If there is no pottage to eat I will dance outside."

"You must behave," said Daama. "Sit. I am tired today."

"But I will dance," insisted the girl.

Daama stood. "Do as I say. I am the best mother ever to exist. I'm also the favourite descendant of the Wind God."

The little redhead looked shocked. Then she giggled again. "You cannot believe that. There is but one God. He has only one Son."

"The Wind God," repeated Daama in a warning tone. "His offspring roam over the plate of the earth and through the dome that is the sky."

"Indeed, little children believe it is a dome." Blanche was serious now. "But in truth, far beyond the sky the stars roam. And as they move they make music in praise of the one God."

Daama seemed choked to silence again.

The little girl ran over to Harsu. "What game shall we play, master lanky-legs?" She stared more closely. "Oh, your poor face. Did you have the smallpox? So did my sister. How frightened I was. It killed my parents. Did you nearly die too?"

Daama's forgetting spell had only half worked. Harsu smiled at Blanche for her kindness—and past sadness. But his mother brought the claw-top out of her apron. It whirled around the girl.

Blanche sank to her mattress. Even drowsing, even with the claw-top so close, words floated out—"Dough-lady ..."

Harsu cleared his throat. "Mother. How will this girl bring you praise?"

"She is pretty. She is lively. Best of all, she is not a boy."

"True." He made his hands into fists to keep himself still. "But in this England a child's meant to be quiet, not to be seen. You criticise when someone else is not logical. But is it sensible to steal this child?"

His mother bared her teeth. "I have praised you on occasion. That does not mean you can imply I make mistakes."

A shout burst out of Harsu. "You can't keep doing this!"

She grabbed a raw egg from the bowl and crammed it whole into her mouth.

His stomach heaved but he said, "Let the little girl go."

Daama spat out the shell. "You are the child. I am the parent. I decide."

She reached out a hand and the claw-top sped into it. Around the room she paced, muttering, scowling.

At last she tugged her white bonnet off and threw it down. Snarling, she ground into it with her heel.

"In this England I can never shine. This was never the place for me."

She gestured. There was a heavy thud in the pantry nook. A third prison-jar stood with the others.

"Not for the girl!" Harsu yelled.

Daama pointed a sharp claw. "Ready the cart or you are next."

"Do it!" he shouted. "Put me in a jar too. Just dare!"

All Daama did was laugh at him. "If you are in a prison-jar, how can you push the cart?"

I can run, Harsu told himself, *Ragnar can look after himself.* But the little ones couldn't. He had to stay. He had to show he was better than his relatives.

With one of her signs Daama charmed the crate with the broken pottery back onto the cart. It must be important if she still didn't trust him to lift it.

All the way to the cavern his mother saved her strength and kept the claw-top whirling around the cart. There was no chance to free the others, nor to escape himself.

Harsu hauled the cart into the Ferry Gate and slumped against the wall. The onager shlopped up to nudge him.

"Get off," he said.

The onager snorted and settled in the shadows again.

Harsu sensed his mother come near. He lifted his head.

She knelt in front of him. "You want me to be happy," she said.

He wanted a mother who wasn't a werestoat.

She touched his hand. "We will find somewhere life will be easier."

For a moment he looked into her eyes. "No more stealing children or babies," he said.

She gave a nod. "I have three children now with perfect looks. When we're settled I shall easily deal with their awful behaviour. For a while I'll be content with a better house in a much better time and place."

She kissed her finger and dabbed his forehead. Did he believe her? He didn't know. He supposed he had to.

She took fifty paces further into the Gate than ever before. Now and then came a flash from the eye of a carved figure or the blade of a sword, or from things for which Harsu had no name. There were buildings that Harsu hadn't noticed the other times: small houses and larger ones, towers and palaces. There were strangely shaped carriages, some high up as if they flew in the dome that was the sky. There were all sorts of scribbles, but Harsu couldn't tell how much of it might be writing.

Daama ended her whispered chant of eyes and time, heart and place.

The spinning began, and turned the sparkling into a web, a glittering network, a shining blur.

The whirling outside the Gate went on for ages. Just as Harsu began to think it would spin forever, his senses jolted. His vision cleared.

FLIP-BEETLE & HEDGE-PIG

THE GLOW OF LIGHT IN THE NEW CAVERN OUTSIDE the Gate was fitful and flickering. Daama stood up. Her lips were painted red, her eyelids blue. Her cheeks had smudges of pink dust. On her head sat a purple cap. Under a red coat, tight trousers were tucked into high-heeled boots. A bag with metal studs hung on her shoulder. She stuffed a roll of parchment into it and glanced at Harsu.

"It is small-minded to stare at new fashions," she said.

As she'd done before, she tossed him a bundle of clothes. He climbed into new trousers, dark green, thick and soft with a stretchy waistband. He liked them. There was a striped top with long sleeves. Dark-blue shoes fastened with a piece that stuck to a matching piece—what a useful idea.

"It's called Velcro. Stop admiring yourself. Hurry up." Daama picked her way out of the Gate.

Harsu burned to see this better time and place. But he might never see the war-steed again. He stayed to stroke its muzzle and rub its black strip of mane. "I'm sorry. Will you be all right?" he asked.

It shlopped ahead of him out of the Ferry Gate and nosed about near the edge of the shore.

The sweet sea had become shallow. Two rowboats rested at the waterline. In the new grove grass rippled and shone. Despite the flickering light, the silver trees bore many copper leaves, even tiny flowers.

"Hurry up," Daama called, already so far ahead she was out of sight.

He ducked back for the cart.

Beyond the grove he stopped and rapped Ragnar's prison-jar. "All my mother wants from you is good behaviour. In a year or less, you and I can be off on those adventures."

Silence in the container.

Harsu flexed his right fingers. That was the waking sign. Would it work faster if he widened his fingers like this …

A curse echoed in Ragnar's jar. "Vittle-besom, child-stealer." The boy's fingers clutched the rim.

"Stay down," said Harsu.

But Zamuna was struggling up in his jar too. "My hair's mussed. I'll look so ugly."

"I'll make sure of it!" cried Ragnar. He wriggled right out, fell slap on the cavern floor and threw a handful of dirt.

Zamuna bellowed and leapt off the cart. Yelling, the two set at each other.

"Why am I stuck in here?" screamed Blanche from her jar. "Let me out. I want something to eat! Fie on this skirt, I am stuck."

"Stop," Harsu cried at them. "Ragnar, stop."

"Grab fun while you can," shouted Ragnar.

"You said you were biding your time, hoarding your strength." Harsu made a snatch for him.

Ragnar whacked Harsu's chest, then dived at his knees and knocked him down. "Bide time and have fun while you're doing it."

"I said, I am stuck!" Blanche shouted again. "Look at me! Help!"

Daama came running back, rummaging in the shoulder bag. She pulled the roll of parchment out of it, a brush and comb, jewels ...

Blanche's jar toppled off the cart, bounced and knocked Daama over.

"She's a flip-beetle." Blanche laughed. She scrambled free of the prison-jar, then reached back into it.

Harsu found he'd gripped the girl's arm. "Run while she's grounded. Run!"

"Let me go," Blanche cried. "I must have my doll."

"Harsu, keep hold of her." At last Daama had the claw-top.

It hummed in its sickening breeze. Ragnar fell flat again. Zamuna collapsed.

Blanche folded up. The poppet fell from her hand. "Pox

on her," she mumbled. "She is naught but a bug-munching hedge-pig …" Then she was asleep.

Daama hissed like a stoat. "How in the universe did I wake the brats? All this hard work. It's almost too much for me."

Harsu kept his head down. Once again she must have thought he'd been trying to catch the little girl when he'd been hoping to save her. This time, he didn't know why he'd told Blanche to run. Daama had promised this was to be a better place and better time, and he believed her.

But she continued. "Ungracious girl. Ungrateful boys. Put them all back in the prison-jars. Hurry with it. Good. Now leave them here."

She scooped up the claw-top and strode on.

Her voice echoed back. "I said hurry. It isn't far."

MY SPIRITS RISE

For a moment Harsu was motionless. leave the children here, underground—Daama couldn't mean she'd store them in the cavern forever.

No—if their new home wasn't far, she'd just be waiting for the best time to fetch them. All the same, he had to force himself to follow the sound of his mother's tread.

The path ended at a wide flight of steps carved in the rock.

"Above is a village: Redbridge," Daama said. "The country is called New Zealand."

What happened to the old Zealand?

Taking a breath of excitement, his mother hugged her shoulder bag. The parchment rustled. "My son, never underestimate the benefit of preparation."

Maybe she meant the curly English he'd seen her writing on the parchment was spells and instructions. He might get a chance to see. The godlet-drops fizzed, and he started to feel quite a bit better.

Her boots rapped ahead on the steps. Halfway up, the stone became narrow wooden stairs riddled by worm holes. At the top Daama grasped a handle and a door creaked wide.

Harsu's spirits plummeted.

Feeble light came through cobwebs over dirty windows. There were holes in the walls, and ragged edges where smaller rooms had been knocked into a single big one. It had never been finished. Against the back wall a long counter had a basin set into it—the kitchen, Harsu guessed. A low partition divided it from the rest, where drifts of sawdust lay on the floor, over a window-seat with missing panels, on broken chairs and a table with only three legs. A door with a cracked cloudy pane led out to a long porch. Another door half off its hinges led to a dark hall with a big door at the end where patches of light came through sections of red and blue glass.

Daama seemed frozen. Then she gave a wail. "This is too much. I can't go on." She sank down weeping.

She kept sobbing as if she were broken. He glanced around again. Perhaps outside the cottage would be better.

He stepped onto the long porch. The air smelled fresh. Warm sun. Clear blue sky. Hills lay on one horizon. From another came the roar of waves. Another roar sounded somewhere, then faded fast.

The garden was tufts of grass and straggles of weeds. A high hedge surrounded it. Behind the hedge rose a pointed turret—the house next door. From where Harsu stood, cracked and overgrown paving led to the front of the cottage and on to a wooden gate.

Something large roared again and flashed by beyond the gate. It seemed to be a sort of carriage with four wheels. But Harsu didn't see any animal harnessed to it. He stepped down to the paving to make out the road better: it wasn't dirt or cobblestones but smooth and black.

Another growling sound swelled so loud that Harsu ducked. Over the road an enormous windowless vehicle grumbled to a halt. He didn't dare move. A huge lever at the back of the thing grabbed a bin as large as one of Daama's storage jars, raised it high and emptied the contents into the carriage.

The vehicle rolled on. Harsu counted eight wheels. Then he heard the same bumps and groaning as before. It was feeding itself from another bin.

He was shaking. The magic in Zealand was far greater than Daama's. Why in all the universe had his mother thought this was the place for them? Zealand was no place for the children either. But nowhere was, except their homes, and they could never return there.

He edged back inside. Daama still wept, hunched over, skinny and small. Harsu had never seen her like this before. He sank next to her. "Mother, hush. After all, this is just a beginning."

Daama slumped against him. Tears dampened his shoulder.

"Mother, we must have great courage. You need to recover. Please rest. The daughter of the daughter of a child of the Wind God can turn this hovel into a palace."

She caught back a sob. "You believe in me."

He found himself hugging her. "We've come all this way. We can't be beaten."

She steadied. With his help she climbed to her feet and wiped her face.

"My relatives threw me out of the place where I was born. Then they forced me to leave my palace and my husband's grave. But my son has faith in me." She raised her arms high. "From the fiasco of my blighted past, my spirits rise. Here at last I will create a palace to make men weep with envy. Women will plead to become my friend."

Harsu took a breath of relief. She hadn't exactly told the truth but she did want praise only from grown-ups.

"My son," she continued, "you have given me the strength to explore the village."

"But it's dangerous," he said. "I'd better come with you."

She gave another sob that was partly a laugh. "No. You can unload every cart from the Ferry Gate. Then stack each bundle in the silver grove. It must be tidy. Do not rush. Take special care of that crate. You know the one. I do not want anything else broken, thank you."

He tensed a little. But she laughed again and patted him.

Harsu slid down the stairs to the cavern and loped through the gloomy maze. He faltered when he reached the cart and the prison-jars. But for now, they must stay where they were. He ran on.

In the cavern the war-steed glanced up, then kept munching the silver grass.

Taking his time, Harsu unloaded the other sixty-nine carts from the Ferry Gate. Off them he took each bundle of finery, each box of slippers and sandals encrusted with jewels, the bowls of copper and marble, cups of silver and gold and whatever else. Chests of all sizes and materials, carved wood, enamel, ivory. One thousand table mats. The crate with the broken pottery.

As carefully as if it held a baby, he placed it down. Inside, the pieces shifted and scraped. And something had rustled. It held parchment now as well as pottery? But the lid was sealed. Daama would know if he tried to open it.

His muscles ached but the godlet-drops simmered.

Back he loped through the cavern and stopped at the prison-jars. He felt the pieces of lentil and the shape of his father's arm-ring in the pouch of the cloak.

"Somehow I will be a man soon," he said. "I want to be a good man like my father."

BOWL OF ASTONISHMENT

HARSU OPENED THE LANDING DOOR. FOR A MOMENT IT was like coming into another new world. The room was transformed.

Daama was smiling again. And once again she wore a new garment. It came only just past her knees. She had black leggings now and soft slippers.

"You're just in time," she said. "I've been out and I've been busy. Admire my handiwork."

This must be like a Zealand palace. Three round globes glowed in the ceiling, one for each part of the large room. He'd need a long pole to reach them and set the oil burning. New white cupboards gleamed in the part that was the kitchen. Blue and white crockery sat on shelves. That big silver box must be an oven. It had a window that showed racks inside. Good idea. Whoever was cooking could see if the pastry burned before their nose said, *Fool of all fools, you've done it again.*

He kept gazing around. The window-seat was polished wood now, with a long comfortable cushion. A big dining table had four stout legs and eight chairs. The floor was tiles which reached through to the kitchen.

But thick carpet lay in the last part of the room which had cabinets, side tables, three soft sofas, and a round table in the middle with a statuette of the Wind God.

"All on my own, I've made a start," she said. "In time I will gain everything that is right and good in this new world. Behold."

She darted to the kitchen and turned a metal spout over a wide basin set into a new counter. The spout gushed water.

Water brought by pipes inside a house—this was extraordinary. Only the King and the very rich could afford this. Even Daama's old palace had not been so fortunate.

"But behold again." She twisted the spout in another direction. The water began to steam—it was hot!

"Such magic," Harsu whispered.

"Indeed, magic is how I did it. The people who live here achieve it by something called plumbers. It's all in here." Daama pointed to a couple of slim glossy books that lay near the Wind God figure. On one he saw the picture of a fine house.

She opened a white door into the hallway. It had been so dark. Now lights like half-moons glowed on fresh cream walls and four closed doors.

With a proud tilt of her head, Daama showed him into one of the rooms. It had walls of blue tiles. There was a mirror where Harsu saw how awkward he looked, and how thin. There was a bath where hot water or cold could spurt again at the turn of a spout. Yet another spout sat over a higher basin. It had drawers under it to hold things like spare soap and even razors, he supposed, when he came to need them.

Daama pressed a silver button in the basin to show how water could be kept in to form a pond, then pressed again so the pond gurgled away. "Here you may wash your hands and face."

There was a cubicle tall enough to wash Harsu standing, with a high spout that sent down warm rain.

Next to the basin was a puzzling large bowl with a double lid. She lifted the smaller top lid. The one beneath had a hole in it. Water already sat in the bowl.

"Why?" he asked.

His mother flipped his ear. "It's the fashion. Stand before it with both lids up, or sit when needful on the one with the hole. When you push this button on the tank above, the bowl fills again with clean water. What do you think?"

He took a moment to find his answer. "Mother, I can say nothing. I am speechless."

BRIGHT IDEA

I HAVEN'T THE TIME OR ENERGY TO RENEW THE WHOLE house yet," said Daama. "That will come when the moon wanes again and I have rested. And, of course, once I've found a steady supply of eggs. But in the end I'll make it all magnificent."

Harsu glanced at the other doors. The room behind the gleaming gold one was sure to be hers. He bet it was already enchanted inside to be more than gorgeous. And fair enough, she had worked hard.

She danced back to the living area, so he snuck a look in the other rooms. They were both shabby and damp.

He found his mother on one of the sofas, turning pages of the glossy books. The covers had English words, rather different from the English of Blanche's time. On one he managed to read: *House. And. Gar-den.* Another word was *New.* The next and last began with *Ze* then *a* then *land*—it must be *Zealand.*

On the front of the second book was an elegant woman, chin up in one of Zamuna's favourite poses. The word on this book was a hard one: *F* then *a*, then *s* and *h*—the sound must be *faa … sh …* the word was *fashion*.

Daama noticed him. "Sticky-beak, these are my magazines, not for you."

She rose and fetched a golden bowl from the kitchen. It was full of eggs. Then she sat back with the magazines and turned a page.

How did New Zealanders make such shiny parchment? It must take a scribe years to ink so many tiny words and draw the colourful pictures. He squinted at a folded-back page. *Ex …* He shook his head and tried again. *Ex … er … cise*—Ah. *Exercise gear for you and your child.* He thanked the godlet-drops.

Daama took an egg from the bowl and licked it straight out of the shell. Fair enough to that, too: she had to recover. But he still couldn't bear to watch.

"You're bothering me," she said. "Go and weed the paving, I'm too tired just yet to bother with the outside."

Outside. He didn't want to go. But his father had been a warrior and his mother had braved the terror of the roaring carriages on the road outside so surely he could weed inside the gate.

—

Gradually Harsu cleared the paving from the porch to the front corner of the cottage. He learned not to recoil when a carriage whooshed by. But how come none of them needed animals?

Another roar choked to silence near the gate. He stayed in a crouch. A vehicle with no roof and only two wheels, one behind the other, and still no animal to pull it, bore two people. How in the universe had they not fallen off? They wore round helmets—they must be warriors.

The smaller figure unbuckled its helmet. Dark-brown hair tumbled down. It was a girl. She swung a leg to dismount. She was more lively and confident than Ragnar or Blanche, more beautiful than Zamuna.

Faintly Harsu heard her: "See you soon, Dad."

Again the English was different from the English of Blanche's time. But he had understood. The girl dashed away. Footsteps crunched on the other side of the hedge.

The man twisted something on the handle of the two-wheels and it roared off.

In moments the girl sped past again on a low board, pushing with one foot. A woman with curly brown hair who must be the mother came running, laughing and calling her. The girl zoomed back and circled her, then together they were out of sight.

Harsu started to grin. This New Zealand—"My mother was right to come," he breathed. "Parents and children, fantastic metal steeds. One day she and I might ride one of our own—*exercise gear for you and your child.* Why can't it be exercise gear for all your children? Me, Ragnar and Blanche. And even Zamuna."

Inside, hoping to see the family again, Harsu sat on the window-seat for a view of the gate.

Daama was flicking through the *House and Garden*. "Coffee machine—I must have one. And a fridge, soon. Oh, this chandelier! It is outstanding. No. I should rest. I charmed up lights for this room only today." She glanced at the globe above the sofas. "But I absolutely deserve something better."

Harsu watched her hands make a complex sign. One moment the globe already in the ceiling gleamed like an eye. Next moment it was replaced by a dazzle of intricate silver with blue and gold stars.

Without thinking, he repeated her sign. On the instant, a second chandelier, twice as dazzling with twice the number of stars, hung over the dining table.

Daama crowed. "I'm stronger than I knew!"

He nearly said it was him, though he could hardly believe it. Yet—however it had happened—the magic had put his mother in an excellent mood. This was a good time to do something for the stolen children.

"In this magnificent kitchen, you're sure to bake the most remarkable creations," he said. "Under these astonishing clusters of light, your three perfect children will understand how deeply their superb mother is owed words of thanks."

She gave a lovely smile and put down the magazine. Then she glided to the kitchen cupboards. "You may be right. Harsu, fetch the prison-jars up to the landing."

Oh. All those stairs.

His mother smiled. "Poor lad. You're worn out." She thought for a moment, then she signed a small beckoning and he found himself gripping the handle of a metal trolley. Well, yes, it wasn't much, but it would make the steps easier. He clattered it down to the cavern, then loaded the cart with the prison-jars and pushed it to the foot of the steps.

"You may not believe me," he whispered while he was tying Blanche's jar to the trolley, "but New Zealand has greater magic than any of us have ever seen or imagined. When Daama asks, say the words she wants to hear and she'll reward you."

"Swear words," Blanche mumbled. "Bite my thumb. I want my poppet."

But at last the three jars sat on the landing behind the kitchen door. Before he opened it he signed two charms over them: *be calm. Be cheerful.*

Pride and excitement swelled up within him. He was son of Mistress-princess Daama, Demon-wizard.

PART THREE

★

THE PERFECT CHILD

PLAYING WITH FOOD

DAAMA HAD MAGICKED HERSELF ANOTHER GOWN from the magazine. The skirt reached the floor, with ruffles like a flower. Her cheeks were plump as buns.

Harsu bowed. "Mother, the god is surely at the pinnacle of pride with his descendant."

Smiling, she tied on the whitest of aprons. On the table she set three looking-cakes—three! One was dark brown. "This is *chocolate*," she said, "it's sweet and rich. It is said that children adore it." The second was decorated with a gold ribbon like a gift ready for opening. The third resembled a cluster of butterfly wings.

She marched to the landing and flicked her fingers. The jars tipped to and fro as the children climbed out.

He'd expected them to be happier. Their movements were slow and tired.

It must be because of the claw-top. Each time Daama used it, Harsu was sure it drained more life from them.

Had they been able to hear his encouraging words when he brought their jars up?

Or had he signed *sleep* instead of *calm*?

Out of his mother's sight, he went through the movements—he wasn't sure.

Daama pointed Zamuna to sit in front of the chocolate cake, Ragnar the cake like a gift and Blanche the cake with butterfly wings.

"Zamuna, begin," Daama commanded.

"Daama is … she is … I forget." The little boy sulked.

Daama gave him only a gentle jab with the gold server.

"Ragnar. You will do better."

He slouched. "I've had worse than anything you can do."

Daama chuckled. "Still my risk-taker." She jabbed him anyway.

"Give me something to take away the taste of the disgusting pellet," he groaned. "Or *phtt*, just beat me again, see if I care."

Blanche was eyeing the boys and cakes, yawning and frowning.

Be careful, Harsu breathed. Then he remembered—this was the first time she'd even seen a looking-cake. She didn't know the rules.

"Mother?" he said.

She took no notice. "Now, my flame-haired girl, do your best."

"Thank you, kind madam," began Blanche.

Daama's cheeks became plumper with satisfaction. Harsu calmed down.

Then Blanche rolled her eyes. "You saa-aaved me, you are remaa-arkable. I'm supposed to be graa-aateful when you made me lose my best poppet that I made my very self ..."

She'd ruin everything! Harsu signed *wake* as hard as he could.

At the same moment Daama raised the server and slammed it down.

Blanche ducked under the table. The server whacked the butterfly cake. It shot off the plate, fell to the floor and broke into lumps.

"Fire and rage!" bellowed Ragnar. He lunged and hurled a chunk at Zamuna. Screaming and laughing, Blanche tossed a lump back at him. Zamuna leapt for the chocolate cake, stuck a hand in it and with a wild shout flung some at Harsu.

The shriek of a stoat cut through the war-cries and laughter. "Good children must be emblems of pride on their mother's brow!"

"You're not the mother of any of us," Blanche shouted. "Only of Harsu."

A growl sounded in Daama's throat. The room filled with a bitter scent. From somewhere she brought the dark wooden top, clutched in a hand that turned into a paw, fingers into black claws. She threw the top hard.

"Enough," she cried. "Stuff the brats back in the prison-jars. I will hang them forever in cages underground."

Guilt pressed on Harsu again. He'd caused this disaster with his confusion of signs, the wrong ones and at the wrong moment.

He did his best to tuck each of the children into the urns in restful positions. A faint curse still echoed from Blanche—*codswallop*; a faint drumming of Ragnar's heels—*ba-ba-bom*.

A last tuft of fur twitched under Daama's chin. She grabbed the lids of cauldrons and clashed them like cymbals. Muscle stood out on her human arms. "I saved them from terrible parents. But see how they thank me."

Words were the only weapon Harsu could use to help the others.

"Mother, the uncountable drops in the underground ocean would never be enough tears of sorrow for how they treat you."

She crashed the lids again. "Everything I've ever done has been for their benefit."

"Yes, you saved them from unkind and indulgent parents," he lied. "Yet something is wrong. They're out of control. Even worse, they've turned into shadows of what they used to look like."

She held the lids as if to smash them over his ears.

He didn't hesitate.

"I saw something in your magazine about children and exercise. That would be an idea. You know, fresh air, harmless running about in this secluded garden. Nobody would see. It could be good for them. But I shouldn't have any opinion. You're the expert."

For a moment she didn't move. Then she lay on a sofa and clasped a lid like a battle-shield over her chest. "I'm more exhausted than any mother ever under the dome of the sky. Give me peace and quiet. Let me think."

That night Harsu curled up on the landing beside the prison-jars.

"How many times must I tell you, for your own sakes, just do what she asks," he whispered.

Then he knelt up. The godlet-drops offered him words: "But if she ever lets you outside, grab the first chance you have. Dash for the road and keep running."

No sound at all came from the prison-jars.

CLAW-TOP

HARSU SPENT THE NEXT MORNING TOILING OVER strong-smelling cauldrons and ladling relish into tiny containers. Every groan that refused to stay inside he forced into lies: "I'm such a lucky boy. It would be bliss to be worthy of such a mother."

He scrubbed so many bowls they seemed endless, even though he used the hot-and-cold spout of New Zealand.

At last he'd washed the final pot.

"Outside," said Daama.

He trudged down to the paving. A haze hung in the sky like a pot-lid.

His mother's voice made him startle. "Stand there by the corner of the cottage."

Here she came leading the children. They squinted in the daylight and huddled together. He was sure of it: the claw-top was sapping too much life out of them. How he hated it.

He mouthed at Ragnar the words that last night had come from the godlet-drops. *Grab the first chance you have. Dash for the road and keep running.*

His mother pointed to the hedge around the cottage. "That is the boundary. I have charmed it so you cannot pass. I've charmed the gate too. Harsu stands there to make sure none of you go near it. I wish nobody to set eyes on you till you're a credit to me. Now go on, play."

The stolen children stared in bewilderment.

She flung her hands in the air. "Jump. Run about."

After a moment Ragnar set off lurching through the long grass on stiff legs. Blanche hiked up her blue skirt and stumbled a step. Zamuna tried a swagger.

Harsu stood ready. If one of them rushed his way, he'd pretend to trip up. But he'd have to charm the gate to open. Would he manage? He glimpsed Zamuna's headband through a tree bearing wizened lemons. For a moment Ragnar balanced on one leg, then toppled over. Blanche grabbed the branch of a tree but dropped back at once.

Liven up, Harsu urged silently. *Come this way.*

Blanche gathered her skirt in her hands. A little faster now, she ran for the lemon tree. Back she came, glanced past Harsu and raced straight at the gate. He braced himself to make the fake fall. But her skirt slipped from her hand. She sprawled on the paving. With a cry she gripped one of her wrists. Blood smeared her sleeve and down her skirt.

Harsu took a step, but Daama was there already. She raised the little girl to her feet. Though Blanche tried to pull free, Daama bundled her onto the porch.

Ragnar hesitated, grabbed Zamuna's hand, they came pelting at Harsu …

On the instant Daama reared up, a stoat-demon with claws and fangs. "Never dare!" she cried.

Zamuna stumbled. Ragnar bent to yank him up again.

The stoat-demon shrieked and threw the claw-top. With the stink of pitch and honey, it circled the stolen boys and Harsu as well. His leg muscles felt glued, his eyes were dizzy. The drag of its spinning was far worse than he remembered, so awful he wanted to die. It circled and circled, herding them to the cottage, up the steps, inside.

Then the top released him. Harsu staggered.

When he straightened, in front of the prison-jars on the landing, the stoat-demon was Daama again. The children stood with their hands palms up in praise. Blood trickled from Blanche's wrist. As he watched, Daama signed a charm over it that looked like a pinch, a sort of gathering motion. The blood—the wound itself—vanished.

"Praise me," said Daama.

In lifeless voices the stolen three began to chant. *"Daama protects us. We are wicked to disappoint her. She has suffered remarkable sorrow but Daama is kind."*

SIZE ARMY?

NIGHT TIME. THE COTTAGE WAS QUIET. HARSU LAY beside the silent containers till the line of light under the kitchen door disappeared.

He fished some scraps of cloth, string and straw from under his shirt, listened again for any sound, then scrambled up. "Blanche," he whispered, and dropped the scraps down to her. "Make more poppets. Imagine dancing and swearing. Never give up. I'll do my best to get you out of here."

He thumped a soft fist on Ragnar's jar. "Practise the cow-flute. Think, where will you go and have adventures when you're free again?"

Ragnar shifted inside. "What about you?" he mumbled.

"Who knows," Harsu replied.

He slapped the last prison-jar. "When you're free in New Zealand everyone will say you're horribly handsome."

"First-rate good-looking …" muttered Zamuna.

Harsu lay down again with his father's cloak and rubbed

the discs between finger and thumb. Though he might never be able to read the markings on them, each felt like an encouraging message.

Even so, the night seemed to take forever while he remembered his fever-dreams.

Harsu finally woke to a fierce hissing in the kitchen.

He found Daama haggard and skinny, almost a skeleton. Draped in a sleeping-shawl from long ago, she propped herself on the counter in front of a new red machine. That's what was hissing. Dark stuff poured into a cup from a tiny pipe.

She took a sip. "Good coffee. But I must have eggs fast. I need seven dozen."

What was dozen? As if he cared. All he wanted was time alone in the house to think, to figure out what to do.

She pointed to an upright silver cupboard. He hadn't seen that before either. "This is a *fridge*. In it, one may store many items that need to be cool. Such as eggs. But I will have to see if I prefer them warm from the nest. You can wait for breakfast ..." She stopped. "No. Even when she badly needs to rest and cosset herself, a mother must put her child first."

Hadn't she said she was off to buy eggs? That wasn't resting.

But on the hob she placed a skillet. With her own hands she took the last egg from a bowl in the fridge and whisked it with a drop of sweet-smelling extract, a nip of cinnamon and milk from a container. She dipped two thick slices of bread in the mixture. Then she dropped them into the skillet and turned them over when the first sides had browned.

With her own hands again she set a plate in front of Harsu. "French toast. Eat."

He went to take a slice in his fingers.

"Oh, wait," she said. "Cutlery. It's the fashion here, don't ask me why." She rattled in a drawer and gave him a blunt knife and small trident, though it had four prongs instead of three so it must be called something different.

New Zealand was indeed strange. The cutlery made eating take longer. But that wasn't entirely a bad thing. The toast tasted wonderful.

He couldn't help smiling at his mother. "Thank you. Supreme breakfast."

"Of course." Daama smiled back. "And now you're going shopping."

What? Him?

"At the gate, turn for the sound of the sea," she continued. "Take the third road on the left. Along there is the mini-mart."

Go on his own? To the where?

Her smile was vanishing. "For the sake of the universe. A mini-mart is a shop. Take the little cart waiting on the porch. My need is growing since you've just eaten my last egg."

Every drop of his blood had started to fizz. "But—but how many?"

"Seven dozen! *Ach*, it means eighty-four. Break even one and know my wrath." She slunk to the window-seat.

The cart at the porch door was so small that Harsu blinked. It was no more than a bag with two wheels. On its little handle, red ribbons fluttered. Bells dangled and chimed as they used to on the harness of her onager.

He wasn't sure about this. But it must be the fashion.

As he reached the gate it swung open, then closed behind him.

Harsu was out on his own for the first time in maybe seven thousand years. Though in his actual life it had been only a few weeks. The last time had been when he found his father's arm-ring in the thicket. It had lain beside his father's statue.

"No," he found himself whispering. His breathing heaved. "It wasn't a statue. It was my father. Daama did it to him. She turned him to sandstone." At the thought—the memory—the truth at last behind his fever-dreams— he almost fainted.

But Harsu made himself stay upright. What Daama had done to his father could not be undone. He had to crush down the memory of his father striding like a king. Right now there was no help for it. He had to go on.

Tall poles lined each side of the smooth black road, wires slung between them. He had no idea what they were for. But here and there a bird perched for a moment before flying again.

A black self-propelled carriage roared past on the road. A red one came up behind and zoomed ahead. By the third carriage—white—Harsu didn't flinch. A yellow four-wheel passed. In the back a boy about Harsu's age gave a silent scream and pointed at the little cart with its bells and ribbons.

Harsu felt himself redden. He'd been right. The shopping cart was a bad idea.

At last he found the mini-mart. The cart bumped the edge of the door and rattled its bells.

Behind the counter, a dark-haired man was talking into his own hand—no, but just as strange he was talking into a small rectangle. He smiled at Harsu.

"I ... am here," Harsu said.

"Mate, that is some trundler." The man put the object down—it shone for a moment then turned dull. Was it magic or machine?

"Are you okay? You look like you're getting over a bit of a shock," he said.

"I ... am here to buy eggs," Harsu stammered. "Seven dozey ... I mean dozen?"

The man pointed to the back of the store.

Harsu clung to the cart. "It is my first time out." Every word made him feel more foolish and more alone.

"Ah, you're the kid from 44 Caddie Street?" The man nodded. "Mrs Daama set up an account. She mentioned she might send a boy. Being new in a place, always a shock eh? So, you're Harsu. I'm Tark."

Tark led him past shelves of bright cans and packets, bins with transparent lids, fridges with transparent doors— his eyes saw but his mind blurred—to a stack of narrow packages. On each of these was the image of a hen.

"No, Sir, she wants eggs," Harsu explained. "Not flattened hens."

Tark gave an odd look. "Comedian, eh? Seven dozen. She must be baking for an army. What size?"

"Size … army?" Harsu asked.

"Oka-ay," Tark said. "I guess size seven." He handed over one of the packets. Now Harsu noticed the bottom was made up of little cradles each shaped like an egg.

"A fool has much to learn, sir." He set the packet in the trundler, his face burning again. He picked up a second package. It slipped but he caught it before it hit the … no he didn't.

Yolk oozed out over the floor.

You will know my wrath if you break one egg.

Harsu felt the blood drain from his face. "I am exceeding sorry."

Tark grinned. "It's hardly the end of the world. Between you and me, let's say the first breakage is on the house."

"Pardon?" asked Harsu.

"That's no charge, and no mention to anyone's mum."

Harsu's heart raced at such thoughtfulness.

Tark wrapped the packets in plenty of paper. "Watch out for cars," he said. A green four-wheel whizzed past. "Like that one, the idiot."

Harsu stepped out of the shop and took a deep breath, dizzy again. He had to pull this shameful cart with seven packets of eggs back to his mother who had killed her husband, his own father.

The ribbons danced. The bells tinkled. At least the road stayed empty all the way to the corner.

But as he turned into Caddie Street a voice called. "Hey!"

On that board with wheels, the girl from next door was rolling towards him.

COSTUME PARTY?

T HE GIRL STOPPED WITH A KICK AT THE BOARD THAT flipped one end into her hand. "You're off school too?"

What should he say? Just ... "Hey."

"So," she continued, "I'm Megan. What's your name?"

"Harsu," he said. "You rode the two-wheel."

"The motorbike, yeah, me and Dad. Harsu, nice name. Hey, I saw the costumes. I thought it was a party. But it's a movie, am I right?"

What was *movie*?

"My room's in the turret next door to you." She grinned. "I wasn't spying much. I'm not so big on the blue dress but I love the Viking get-up. Cool."

She felt cool? To Harsu, the morning was already warm.

"The special effects will be awesome," she went on. "For a minute, wow, that woman in the apron turned into a giant weasel still with the apron."

All Harsu could do was blink.

"That little girl took a bad tumble," said Megan. "Is she okay?"

"Blanche is … okay," Harsu answered.

But Megan frowned. "Those kids look like they can't run to save themselves. Are they useless actors or just acting useless?"

He could hardly understand a thing she said.

"Whatever," she went on, "they need a coach. Wish I could do it. But I'm restricted for another couple of weeks 'cause I've been sick. I'm only allowed the skateboard for twenty minutes every two hours. Time's nearly up. Have you been sick too?"

He shook his head.

She made a face. "Am I being too nosey?"

It seemed best to shake his head again.

Megan clattered the board down and set a foot on it. "The costumes are from everywhere, so I guess it's a time-travel movie. Or it's an ad—" she looked pleased with herself—"like, for some new super-food. Before they have it, the kids are weak as. Afterwards they're superheroes. You were rehearsing the Before bit. Like they'd never done sport in a thousand years."

Harsu gave a choke of surprise.

"So, good acting after all." Megan studied him. "But your face says not. They really stink at sport?"

Stink? Smell bad? She was very puzzling.

"They do not get much exercise at the moment," he said.

"Then I hope someone good is coaching them for the After bit." She waited a few seconds. He shrugged. "Okay, you're only the gofer. You know nothing." She grinned again. "Oh, lightbulb moment. Coaching isn't exercise but it's next-best. I bet I can clear it with Dad."

A whirr and she'd gone in the direction of the mini-mart.

Coaching. Movie and *ad. Gofer.* New Zealand English was the hardest language he'd ever known.

He pulled the trundler of eggs carefully on.

Just before he reached the cottage gate, Megan whirred up again and stopped beside him. In her hand were two small cones.

"I figure you need a reward for dragging the ribbons and bells." She held the cones out. "First choice is yours."

What on the plate of the universe … Harsu took the red one. It was cold.

"*Mmm*, luck-ee, you left my fave." She tore the wrapper off the orange cone and took a nibble.

So it was some sort of treat. Harsu tore off his wrapper then tried a bite. His teeth felt shock, but next moment sweetness poured through him. His eyes watered. "This is food from the gods' table—never have I tasted such a wonder."

Megan's smile grew wide. "Sorry, I was way wrong. You're definitely one of the actors. Wow, so the ad—or the movie—has a heap of gods?"

He was into his third bite. "I don't know *movie*," he said.

138

"You are so funny." Her eyes sparkled. "Now say you've never seen *Star Wars*, go on."

He shot a look upwards. "In the New Zealand universe the stars do battle?"

She laughed and rolled the board on to his gate. He licked the last crumb of the cone before he joined her there.

"Thank you—" he began.

But something buzzed in her pocket. She grabbed out one of those rectangles Tark had talked into. "Oops, Dad's texted, I'm over time. Glad you enjoyed the ice cream."

Megan smiled as bright as the sun, the moon and stars. Then she sped off down her driveway.

A trundler ribbon fluttered up across Harsu's face. The bells tinkled.

"Before now my gullet would have choked on the stones of jealousy. I would have strangled with envy of this girl and her easy life," Harsu whispered. "But here my mother and I will have such a life too ... if I can forgive her for my ..." He tried but couldn't say *father*.

He firmed his shoulders. "I will make sure Daama becomes kind to the stolen children. I will make sure she keeps the stoat hidden."

The gate swung open. He started through.

There on the porch was his mother, still scrawny and hunched. She was staring at the hedge that hid Megan's house.

Harsu neared the steps, heart starting to thump.

Daama began straightening up. "And I might have missed her. Thank you, my son, for keeping the girl talking right at the gate."

On her hands dark stoat fur sprouted. On her face—fur.

"My son," she whispered. "We have indeed arrived in the best place. Already I have seen the child perfect above all others."

The perfect child … The shock of what she meant slammed into him. He had to grip the railing to keep himself steady.

No matter what Daama had promised him, she was a werestoat. She'd be one forever. She'd never change.

GOOD HUNTING

DAAMA GRABBED THE CART WITH BOTH SKINNY hands. "Peel the onions in that sack on the floor," she said to Harsu. She disappeared to her room.

Fists clenched, Harsu sprang to the landing, then signed *wake* over the jars. Nothing happened. He tried again. Nothing.

With his whole arm he signed a furious wake charm straight at Ragnar's prison-jar.

"*Ow!*" Ragnar shouted. "Let me at you!"

"Keep your voice down," said Harsu. "We must act."

"Smoke and rage. Fire!" Ragnar blew a blast on the flute.

"Don't be a fool," said Harsu.

Ragnar blew another blast. "Last night you told me to practise. This is my battle cry—Smoke and rage!"

"Shut up!" yelled Harsu.

The door flew open. There was Daama. With both hands she lashed a sleep charm over Ragnar's urn.

"That was the ruffian's last chance. Perfect boy, *ptah!* He will be sandstone. Harsu, kick the jar down to the cavern."

Harsu had got everything wrong again, so badly wrong.

"Dawdler! Is this yet another job I must do myself?" she cried.

Harsu took hold of the jar and started tipping it gently on its side. "I'm doing it, look."

"I said kick it. The jars are unbreakable. I should know, I made them." Daama slammed the door.

The jar might be unbreakable. But Ragnar wasn't.

"Ragnar," said Harsu. "Ragnar!"

No reply. Was he sandstone already? Harsu swore under his breath.

But surely Daama needed far more strength than she had now before she could use such an enchantment.

"Risk-taker, hoard your energy," he whispered.

He didn't trust the small metal trolley—he'd do better by himself. He wrapped his arms as far around the jar as he could, sat half in front to prevent it from crashing, and kept talking as he eased it down the steps.

"You must climb out. There are boats by the underground sea. Take one. Escape."

When he reached the cavern he peered into the jar. Ragnar was a jumble of limbs. Harsu couldn't tell if he was breathing.

—

Onions. Harsu's eyes and nose leaked from the stinging juice. The one thing worse than peeling onions was peeling them when his stomach felt as if he'd swallowed stones. If only he'd hidden that stupid flute. If he hadn't woken Ragnar in the first place.

A voice cried outside. "Hey! Harsu!"

Megan.

He dropped the knife and ran to the porch.

She waved from the street. On her head was a cap. She wore tight black leggings and bright yellow shoes. "Can I come over?"

That was the worst thing she could ever do.

"No. The gate's stuck," yelled Harsu.

Thank goodness she stepped backwards and disappeared.

But she sped into view again, hurdled the gate and ran to the foot of the porch steps. "Don't tell my parents I did that."

Harsu couldn't help grinning. But she had to leave. "You cannot be here. My mother—let's say right now she is cranky."

"Yeah, they get like that. But so," she went on, "if you guys are up for it I can coach the kids now."

"*Up for it*—I don't know what that means." He glanced around. Still no Daama. "But a *coach* is a carriage to ride in."

"True," Megan said. "A coach is also someone who teaches."

"In this language, one word means too many different

things." He jumped down the steps to shepherd Megan back to the gate.

"I thought you might be new to English." She wasn't budging.

"I am new to New Zealand English. Now, please leave …"

"But *coach*. Weird, eh?" She twisted a stand of hair round a finger and nibbled its raggedy end. "*Hmm*, I guess a coach with wheels carries people. And teaching-coaching is like carrying people in a different way, to help them on further. Anyway, Dad says I'm allowed. Where are the kids?"

Harsu could hardly say one was imprisoned in an underground urn. But maybe he could get the two little ones free now. He'd sort out Ragnar later.

"Wait here." He darted inside. The landing door was open. The faint sour scent drifted around. If Daama was busy down in the cavern …

He made a firm *wake* sign over the two prison-jars. "Come. Play with a girl."

On the instant Blanche was wriggling up.

"Zamuna, come on!"

In moments, the little boy was out too. Blanche grabbed his hand and dashed over the porch, down to the grass, her long skirt swishing. They shaded their eyes, squinting at Megan.

The godlet-drops drummed in Harsu's chest. This must be managed carefully and fast.

"Megan," he said, "this is Blanche and Zamuna. Please, show them how you jump the gate."

But Blanche was gaping at Megan's leggings. "To show so much of yourself is permitted?"

"Why not?" said Megan.

Blanche flung up her arms. "Praise be, the Protector is surely dead."

"Protector of what?" Then Megan grinned. "I bet that's from the script. Where's the Viking kid? First costume choice for being a Viking, I'd take warm undies."

"Oh …" Blanche gripped Harsu's arm. "Where is Ragnar— his prison-jar is not with mine and Zamuna's. What has Daama—?" She stopped, eyes scared.

"There's a lock spell on the gate," he said in her ear. "But hope for the best. Megan will show you …"

At that moment Daama, in a plain skirt and apron, glided out to the porch. Harsu's mouth turned dry. Zamuna and Blanche stiffened.

Megan gave a bright smile but she was looking hard at Daama. "Dad said I could stay half an hour. Is that okay?"

Daama nodded. "You come from next door. You have a father. Where is your mother?"

"She's a lawyer. So's he," said Megan. "They're taking turns for high-powered meetings. She's back on Friday."

"So your father is home at this moment." Daama looked hard back at Megan, from the yellow shoes to the ends of her brown hair. "Very well. You may stay in the garden. For half an hour."

Her smile was welcoming.

But as she walked inside, so plump that she waddled, she bent to Harsu and murmured, "Good hunting takes patience and time."

LICKINGS

Harsu gripped blanche's hand. "it's okay," he murmured. "Daama's watching so we'll just have fun."

"I have doubt." Blanche clenched her jaw.

Megan's face sparkled. "Okay. You guys look terrific. But let's face it, that's not enough if you're actors. While not to boast, I was sprint champ last year even though I was a junior. So, you two little ones …"

"I am not little," said Zamuna.

"Nor am I," said Blanche.

"Sorry, you two not-as-lanky-as-Harsu," Megan said. "D'you want to change into sports gear? Wow, top marks for acting baffled, like Harsu and *movies*. Come on—track pants. Not even sneakers?" She wiggled the toes of her yellow shoes. "O-kay. Your feet, your problem. Zamuna, I guess your name is—what, Egyptian?"

"I do not know 'gyptian. I am from Ur." He preened. "I am champion."

Megan bit down a grin. "And you, old-fashioned English-whatever," she said to Blanche. "Let's check out the space."

Harsu trailed with them down the garden. With luck the back boundary might be weaker than the gate. He took a few steps further than the others and tested it. No. It was like a spongy invisible mattress.

"Warm-ups," said Megan. "You'll know about stretches. Let's get into it." She raised her arms over her head.

After a moment Blanche lifted hers.

"Stretch, *pah*." Zamuna folded his arms.

Megan laughed. She took them through arm raises and the little boy joined in at last. Then she broke into gentle running on the spot. "Copy. You too, Harsu."

Zamuna raised his chin. "I am already first-rate at running."

"Sure you are. How old are you, six?" Megan asked.

"I have been seven for a long time," Zamuna answered.

"It always feels like that." She chuckled then set two fingers on her wrist. "Just checking my pulse rate. I've been stuck inside for three whole weeks."

Zamuna and Blanche glanced at each other and almost smiled.

"Strep throat actually," Megan went on. "Mum and Dad are being cautious and boring, which I guess is their job. Hey, Blanche, you look better already for some exercise. Harsu, am I right?"

"Maybe, yes," he said. Blanche's face had flushed peach.

"So." Megan eyed the scruffy yard with its stones, weeds, tufts of grass. "This is not the world's top circuit."

Zamuna's nose was more scornful than ever. "I run over burning sand and sharpest rock."

She bowed, a hand on her heart. "Then a jog to the porch and back should be a piece of cake."

"Cake to eat?" asked Zamuna.

"You guys are cute and so weird," said Megan. "Okay, jog. Nice and easy. No sprinting yet."

Zamuna scoffed but away he went. Harsu couldn't resist racing past him, but he let Blanche speed ahead of them both, skirt hoisted in her hands. She hesitated at the corner of the house and glanced up. Daama's shape moved behind the dining-room window and Blanche turned back.

Harsu made sure Zamuna caught up with him on the turn. They ran back together. Blanche reached Megan again just ahead of them and tumbled laughing in the grass.

"The last time I ran," she said, "it was through the forest. I hid from my guardian."

Megan pulled her up and glanced at her wrists. "Call me a snooper but a hedge is for looking over. Yesterday you took a tumble, but now there's not even a scratch. So it was fake blood. How'd you do that?"

Daama's voice called: "Dear children." She glided down through the grass.

"Don't say the half hour is up already? Or maybe it is." Megan jiggled her knees. "'Scuse me, can I use your bathroom?"

She dashed for the porch.

Harsu flung himself after her, was inside just as Megan opened the landing door.

"Movie props, yay! Ali Baba jars. Obviously not the loo." She darted to the hall. The bathroom door banged.

Heart racing, Harsu glanced around. The kitchen probably looked normal. The table was clear. Not even a small cauldron seethed on the hob.

Daama came in, her hands beginning a complex sign. A blur like a heat mirage hurt Harsu's eyes. He squeezed them shut.

When he forced them open, a new looking-cake sat on the table. Cream oozed between three layers. Its top was circled with a crown of flowers made of icing. The taste must blossom on the tongue of any being, human or god, who might deserve it.

Megan burst back in. "Sorry about that—wow, how stunning is this!" She reached to the glorious cake.

"Don't touch," cried Harsu.

"Course not. But at my house, first to see a drip is allowed." She dabbed the rim of the plate, stuck the finger in her mouth, then made a face. "*A-yuck*, tastes of pine trees. *Duh* to me. It's just a prop."

"There is no more drip," Daama said. Somehow now she held a bowl and spoon. "But here, try the sweet lickings."

Megan blinked, frowning, but her hand started rising to take the spoon.

Harsu knocked her arm. The spoon flew through the air, the bowl clattered to the floor and spun under the table. He grabbed Megan to haul her outside.

But Daama's hand plunged into her apron pocket and brought out the claw-top, ready to throw.

CRACKING

MEGAN!" HER FATHER'S VOICE RANG FROM THE street. "Game over."

With one hand Daama stuffed the claw-top back into her apron. The other hand flicked towards the gate. Harsu heard the click of it opening.

Megan jumped to the porch. "Guess what, Dad, I nearly ate a movie prop."

For a moment Harsu's mother snarled like a stoat. But with a calm human smile she pulled Harsu with her to the porch.

Beyond the gate was the motorbike with Megan's helmet slung on a handlebar. Her father, carrying his own, had just reached the porch steps. His hair was fair, rather like Ragnar's. He gave a puzzled smile at Zamuna and Blanche there on the grass. They stared at him and the helmet and looked afraid.

"Good day," said Daama.

"Hi. I'm Grant from next door. Apologies. I have to gather Megan up for an appointment so we're in a rush. Usually we'd welcome you with a plate of muffins."

"Sorry, Dad. I lost track." Megan jumped down and linked arms with him. "See you guys. Practise the stretches, okay?"

In moments she and her father were past the gate, buckling their helmets. The bike roared off.

The gate was still wide. Blanche shot a look at Zamuna … They ran for it.

But with a smooth flick of her fingers, Daama made the gate latch. She pulled the claw-top from her pocket. It herded Blanche and Zamuna back to the cottage, to the landing, into the prison-jars.

"Toad-lady," Blanche cursed. "Dough-besom-witch …" A little snore echoed.

The fake cake had half vanished from the table. Hasty magic. But Harsu knew not to say so.

His mother eyed him. Harsu couldn't tell if she was angry or not. His mind raced. "The girl's father was nearby. I knew the half hour was nearly over. I tried to be sensible."

"My loyal son—" But Daama was already turning away. "How beautiful that child is. She obeys her parent. She is indeed everything. What praise she will bring me when she is mine."

—

It was another night when Harsu tossed and turned on the landing. Under cover of the cloak, he took out the warrior's arm-ring. He tried it on under his sleeve. It might help him work out a plan.

As he turned again, his foot bumped Blanche's jar. He heard the rustle of her skirt but didn't think she'd woken up. He dropped to sleep at last.

Then he was dreaming about the Chief Cook and all the under-cooks and all the slaves from the oldest and wisest grey-haired to the youngest child, every one of them running away and leaving him.

"There's work to do," Daama called in his dream.

He woke up.

Outside the landing door she shouted again. "I said, work to do."

He still wore the arm-ring. If it dropped down and Daama saw it, at the very least she'd chuck it out. He tucked it back in the pouch, and the pieces of pottery lentil scraped like a raspy whisper. Harsu wrapped the cloak and left it all in the corner behind the jars.

Into a simmering cauldron Daama was adding drops that smelled like foot-rot.

"Don't slack about. Shell these walnuts." She dumped a bag on the counter.

At least it wasn't onions. But the bag was twice as big as Daama's head even when she wore her travel wig.

Her eyes turned narrow and dangerous. "What are you thinking?"

Harsu kept his face straight. "This lowly creature is over-whelmed by the constant astonishment of being thought worthy of helping the most remarkable cook in all the universe."

"As he should be," she said. "Have a bite of breakfast. Then get cracking. That is New Zealand slang for *hurry up*."

"Your sense of fun is as great as your importance," he said.

She didn't look as if she understood. *Cracking? Walnuts? Have you heard of having a joke, being friendly? Do stoats even know the word fun?*

It was a risk but the godlet-drops urged him to speak. "Mother," he said, "it's time I became serious. I want to learn how I might assist you if I were permitted to be a man."

Daama's human shape morphed for a moment into stoat shape again. A look from her beady black eyes fixed on his scarred face.

"How do you think you could help?" she asked.

"To prove my worth I can do small things, perhaps not important things," he said. "But there is that crate below that I handled so carelessly. There is no way I can make amends for my extreme bumble-fingers. But may I humbly ask that I take responsibility and repack it for you?"

Her eyes narrowed even more. "I do not want you in the cavern."

Why not? What was she doing there?

He cracked another walnut. "My mother's word is unbreakable law."

After a moment she spoke again. "I promised the relatives to care for you, which I have done well. I've had no time to teach you anything. There seemed little point. But I daresay you could be bright enough to mend what you broke."

Her fingers, hooked like claws, scratched in the air. Down the hall came the hum of magic and a ruffle of soft bumps and bangs.

When it stopped, she collapsed on a sofa, drawn and pale.

Then she rose and handed him a brush and a large pot. The smell from it made his stomach heave. She tugged him into the hall and opened the room across from the bathroom.

Days ago it had been empty and damp.

Now soft carpet covered the boards. A silver lamp hung from the ceiling. At the window, curtains draped in thick folds. A bed had a large pillow. The blue coverlet was patterned with silver stoat-prints.

On the floor was the crate.

"Do the task I set, here out of my way. It will show me if you can be of real use." With stoat claws she prised off the crate lid.

Inside lay rolls of parchment, dusty tablets of pottery, some whole, many broken, all covered in markings in neat lines and columns, writing from thousands of years in the past. Proper tablets. Not just the lentils for teaching students.

His old cloak was still bundled on the landing with the arm-ring and his own pottery pieces. He had better fetch it as soon as he could.

With a sharp claw his mother reached to stroke his chin. "A parent gives a child half an hour to become familiar with a task. Then there's work in the kitchen. Don't dare glue any piece till you're sure of it. And remember it was hard work creating that bedspread. Don't mess it up."

SPORTS LEGS

WALNUT DUST AND FRAGMENTS OF SHELL LAY ALL over the kitchen counter. Daama stirred a reeking cauldron. But Harsu's mind still stirred through what he'd seen from the crate in the half hour she'd let him have. Pottery dust, shards of tablet. He'd been able to write—or at least copy—three words when he was six, and that had been in Sumerian script. English was easier. He'd already figured out a few words he'd seen in the parchments she'd scribbled on. He'd done the same with words in the magazines. Would it be too difficult for him to learn more …?

Rat-tat sounded at the porch door. Daama looked confused. She clanged a lid on her stew and glided to see who it was.

"Hiya, Mrs Daama. No lawn-mowing yet, eh?" It was Megan. She peered closely at Daama again.

Harsu studied Megan too. She didn't seem harmed by eating that drip of icing. She was cradling a bulky bag.

She wore the same black leggings as yesterday, the same baggy grey top.

"I had to hurdle that gate today too," she said. "Lucky it's my speciality. Okay if I'm here for another half hour?'

Before thinking, Harsu cried, "There are no more jars!"

Eyes hooded, Daama turned and laid a hand on his arm. "There will be no need for another jar," she murmured. "When I have dealt with the father, this girl will behave well, that I promise. Go outside with her."

She shut the door on them.

Megan sat on the steps and put down the bag. "Is she your real mum?"

"Of course." He spoke sharply but wasn't sure why.

"Sorry, we were just wondering," she said.

"Then don't." Harsu had to make her leave and never come back. The only way might be to make her hate him.

The door opened again. Out stumbled Blanche and Zamuna. The door shut.

"Always the costumes," Megan said. "And still no Ragnar —is that his name? I hope his character doesn't die in the movie, eh?" She dropped her bag. "Anyway, let's crack into it."

"Like walnuts," Harsu said.

Megan rolled her eyes. "Like, warm-ups." She started a stretch. "Come on, you little ones look way feeble again."

Harsu made a careful sign of waking. Blanche brightened a little. She tucked her skirts up.

"High time for that," Megan said. "If you're running for your life you don't want a dumb dress in the way."

Blanche smiled up at her. She rummaged in her pocket-pouch and pressed a new straw poppet into Megan's hands. "A token of friendship. Harsu gave me the straw when I was unhappy."

"For me? I'm not much into dolls, but if you made it, that's special." Megan glanced at Harsu. "That was kind of you."

He felt himself blush.

She slipped the doll into her bag. "Now, side-steps. Join in when you're ready." She started off.

Blanche, clumsy at first, soon moved as if she danced. Zamuna began trying to step better than her.

"Now we'll do starting position." Megan crouched and showed them. "Ready—set—go. This one's for fast take-off. Short-distance running."

Zamuna stuck out his chin. "I was training to be King's Messenger."

The little kid was trying to impress Megan. Harsu snorted.

Zamuna stuck his chin higher. "How does the King send news of victories if not by his messenger?"

"Me, I'd go for cellphone," said Megan. "But obviously the movie's before the time of even a landline."

"Landline is for running? I don't understand," Zamuna said. "But I am faster than the King. Yet in only one day he ran from Nippur to Ur and back again."

"That could be so cool if I knew how far it was," Megan said. "Tell me this much, is your set down those stairs?"

"Set is on the grass." Zamuna dropped to a crouch. "Ready. Set."

Megan laughed. "Okay, ready—set—looking good—go!"

Zamuna sprinted for the back boundary.

Blanche took two steps but her skirt came untucked. She stumbled and righted herself. "Fie upon fie!"

Megan pulled some black and orange leggings out of her bag. She tossed them to Blanche. "Try these."

The little girl stared.

Megan seemed especially mischievous. "I'll help you get into them. Race you to the bathroom." She bounced up the steps.

She'd planned this!

But Daama appeared at the porch door and raised a hand. "Thank you, Megan, I will help Blanche change. You go back to the garden."

She beckoned Blanche, Harsu as well, and whispered to him, "Stay there with the girl."

Zamuna came running back and posed in a stretch.

"And keep that brat still," Daama muttered. She passed Harsu the claw-top. At the sight of it Zamuna paled.

How heavy it felt in Harsu's hand, smooth and oily from working its spell.

"I can't use it," he said sharply.

"Of course not," his mother whispered. "It works itself when my own enchantment is at an ebb. But see? The mere threat of it now is enough to control Zamuna."

She led Blanche inside.

Megan's eyes gleamed. "What an idiot. I forgot the matching sweater." She yanked another piece of clothing out of her bag.

In two easy leaps she was on the porch again, past Harsu and into the cottage.

The claw-top began thrumming in his hands.

The godlet-drops felt like bolts of lightning.

"I didn't mean I *can't* use it," Harsu said. "I mean I *refuse*. It will not rule me!"

With all his strength he cast the dreadful thing down the garden.

Then he rushed inside.

There was no sign of Megan. The door to the hall was closed.

But the one to the landing was open wide. Far down he heard her voice echo.

"I was right. Movie set! This is amazing."

PANTRY OF DOOM

HARSU LEAPT DOWN THE WOODEN STAIRS AND THE slippery stone ones. He ran to the first turning in the cavern. "Megan!"

No sign of her. He stared around.

Daama had been working at many changes. The underground maze was rich with the scent of herbs and dried fruit. It smelled of onions, garlic and carrots, even of steam from the fattest pastries just out of the oven. He hurried through the dim light, threading between rows of shelves that hadn't been here before. They groaned with the weight of boxes, bundles and jars of all sizes. As he ran on, the scents soured with whiffs of preservative, the stink of pitch from pine trees.

Pine trees . . . pitch . . . Megan said that's what the icing tasted like. That's what the black pellets had tasted of—the one he knew had stopped him growing, and the second one she'd fed to Ragnar.

Ahead, he heard Megan laugh. "Dad is so wrong. He said this place couldn't have a basement but it's enormous."

"Megan!" shouted Harsu again.

He rushed left, towards the underground sea. The spaces between the stacks widened. These shelves were taller and deeper, crowded with bundles, some bulging down to the floor. He came to a row of huge earthenware containers, empty. His mother had created them ready for who could guess how many more children?

On a shelf behind them, among rows of flasks, sat the poppet Blanche had lost.

Daama had found it. And she hadn't given it back to the little girl. Harsu nearly grabbed it.

But just ahead stood Ragnar's prison-urn. He ran to that instead and stumbled on something.

Another new poppet lay on the floor. Brave little Blanche must have managed to come down in the night, hunting for her own lost doll or maybe for Ragnar. And she'd given this one to Ragnar, for some comfort. That was like her.

And Ragnar had chucked it out. That was like him too.

Harsu snatched up the poppet. "Ragnar?" He rapped hard on the jar.

Nothing stirred.

He dropped the doll back down the neck and sped on to find Megan.

Harsu searched deeper into the cavern. The floor was

piled with all the stuff he'd tidied, the carved lacquered chests, sacks of hessian, bags made of expensive tapestry.

All of a sudden he thought his mother was right beside him. His chest jolted—but it was only one of her head-dresses, in a whole row of them.

On a shelf right ahead were three shapes wrapped in linen. One moment their scent was sweet, in the next came the stink of pitch. It must be the looking-cakes. Each was marked with the five claws of the werestoat. Below the claw marks were other signs—words in sticks and triangles. From the size of each shape he knew what they were. Zamuna's fig cake—the signs must read *Zamuna* and *fig*. The almond cake was Ragnar's—so *Ragnar* and *almond*.

The third shape—it was the first cake in the universe. On it he read the only words he'd ever written himself, on the student's lentil. *Harsu my son*.

But this time his mother had written them. So the cake had been his.

How it hurt to remember what she'd said. *An excellent mother would bake such a treat for the birthday of a child whom she loved beyond measure.* She did love him. But she still wanted a perfect child, and it was never him. He crouched as if he'd been sliced by a sickle-sword.

Harsu forced himself up again to search for Megan. To his left, at last, he heard the lapping of the sweet-water sea.

He swung through the opening. Between the silver trunks of the trees the sea glinted as if light flowed there instead of water. A single rowboat lifted up and down on the ripples. The empty carts were lined up just as he'd left them. The stone Gate of Time and Place, half on the pebbles, half on the rippling sea, seemed to float as if it were parchment. The war-steed rested inside.

He heard the rustle of metal.

"*Ouch*, those leaves are sharp." And there was Megan, sucking a finger.

"You shouldn't be here," he called.

"This place is way-amazing." She pointed to the Ferry Gate. "What's that tunnel? And the donkey-horse thing?"

The onager raised its head. *Dgerr.*

She let out a yelp. "It's not a prop. It's alive! Why is it underground?" She began to pick her way to the Gate.

Harsu ran and gripped her arm. "Go home."

She wrenched away. "I'm only curious."

"Get out!" He grabbed again, she jumped aside, but Harsu lunged. They both slipped.

"All right! I'm gone." She scrambled away.

He pounded after her. She was so fast he didn't see her again till she was past the shelves, almost at the row of jars. She had stopped.

She snatched something up. The new poppet. Ragnar must have tossed it out a second time.

Then came a faint fart from the cow-horn flute.

Megan glanced around. She placed a hand on the rim of the jar.

"No!" Harsu dived for her.

Too late. She was peering in.

"Ragnar?" She dropped back, stared at the walls and cavern roof. "There's not even a camera. This isn't a movie. What's your mother doing with these kids? I'm getting Dad!"

She dropped the doll and raced for the stairs.

SPIT UPON HUMANS

HARSU SPED AFTER MEGAN. SHE LOST HER FOOTING ON the stone steps but scrambled on. When he reached the kitchen, Daama and Blanche were teetering as if a whirlwind had spun past them.

Running footsteps crunched on the drive next door.

"Dad!" Megan was shouting. "Dad!"

Daama prodded Harsu. "Quick. Where's the claw-top?"

"I threw it aside," he said.

"Impossible." She prodded again. "Where is the top?"

"Somewhere in the grass."

She thrust her hands into her hair and gnashed out curses. "How could he throw it? I've taught him nothing ..." She stopped and listened.

Then she rushed outside and fetched Zamuna. She bundled him and Blanche into the prison-jars, slammed the landing door, and tossed some magazines on the dining table.

"The human father is coming." She signed for the gate to open. "Harsu, flick through a magazine. Look normal."

Normal? He had no idea how he kept in a snort.

Grant's boots thudded up the porch steps. "Hey there, Mrs Daama."

"We're searching for recipes," she said. "But do come in."

Grant nodded, stern but polite. "Megan's upset and I can't get sense out of her. Do we have a problem?"

Daama widened her eyes. "Such drama, every day. That is so like the small rascals for whom we care."

"If you say so." Grant didn't smile. "All I know is something happened in the movie set."

"Movie?" asked Daama. "Set?"

"A boy stuffed in an Ali Baba jar." Grant frowned at Harsu. "Is there some explanation? Where are the kids?"

Daama spread her hands in a gesture that said how could she know?

Buy time, Harsu told himself. If she cast one of her spells on Grant, who would help Megan? "Sir, we were playing."

"The tricks they get up to." His mother's mouth smiled. Her eyes didn't.

"Kids." Grant gave an out-of-shape grin. "I guess she's frustrated and bored. This week she's missing her mum. I'll calm her down, then try again. Sorry to bother you."

"Not at all," Daama said. "A good parent must make inquiries."

"Very true." Grant scanned the room with a blink at the enormous silver chandeliers. "Megan reckons the way to the set is down through the kitchen. These houses don't have basements, not on this land. It's too close to the sea." He glanced at the landing door. "That'll be the laundry or pantry."

Daama chuckled and turned the handle. "As you see."

In a spinning of air, two prison-jars and Harsu's bundled-up cloak were replaced by shelves stocked with cans, boxes and packets. A small bag of onions. A china jar like a pig had a label that Harsu could read. *Cookies*.

Daama lifted off the pig's head.

"The girl has a lively imagination. I welcome such a treasure into my home at any time." She held out a cookie topped with a walnut.

Grant hesitated but accepted it. She kept her hand out till he took a bite, then she flicked her fingers as people do to dismiss a fly. Grant backed out.

Daama held the go-away sign steady till the gate-latch clicked.

The mirage of the pantry vanished. There was the landing again, the prison-jars, Harsu's cloak rolled up in the corner. The scent of honey mingled with the smell of stoat.

"A human man," Daama said with utter scorn. "I spit upon humans. I am divine."

SCRATCH-WRITING

B<small>UT NOW DAAMA CRAWLED TO THE WINDOW-SEAT.</small> She lay down and pulled her apron over her eyes. "You'll have to store Blanche and Zamuna underground, I'm far too tired. I have to decide—statues or stoppers of pitch. Nothing can escape the pitch I make. But statues may be better. I could have them on show."

Harsu forced himself not to shout. He forced himself not to think of his father. "My opinion is worth less than the little toenail on my own dirty left foot. But to store the children forever would be a terrible waste. And statues—that does not seem right for this time and place of New Zealand."

He flexed his fists and kept going. "Forget those children. Leave them where they are for now. It's more important for you to save your strength and think of yourself. In a million ranks of mothers, you stand supreme. People must see proof of your power. Thousands of men and women must come and learn from the mere sight of you."

There was a silence. Then Daama pushed down the apron. "If people saw proof, you say? You have ill-formed ideas, but they're a beginning." She rose to her feet. "I have to move as fast as possible. Now time is against me. I wanted to make this cottage a palace, a feast of visual delight, before taking even the smallest risk."

She'd already taken so many stupid risks ... Harsu tightened his jaw so he'd say nothing.

She was continuing: "... to create three beautiful patios and a central fountain. But it's not a lasting heartbreak. I will have them soon enough."

Now she took his shoulder and examined him from his tangled hair to his lanky legs. "Maybe. It is worth a try. As I keep saying, the perfect mother always gives time to her child. A child who is ready to grow."

Grow. She meant him. Inside him was a lurch of hope that the spell of the pitch-pellet would be reversed.

"It's even more important now that you sort my lists, recipes, my charms and records. We have three days. Look here." She scratched four sets of symbols on a piece of paper. Two were in the sticks and triangles his father had used. Two were in English. "Concentrate. You must recognise them and match them. These ones are English for *sandstone* and *statue*," she said, pointing to each. "And these mean *sandstone* and *statue* in the signs of Ur. I want every tablet, every piece of parchment that bears these words."

"Why?" said Harsu, though he hoped he knew the answer.

"Does every boy keep asking questions?" she snapped. "It is many years since I worked that enchantment. I must be sure what to do if I decide to use it again. I remembered some of the steps and wrote them in English but I must check against the old tablets. Be especially careful with any that you broke by your clumsiness. Paste them well."

Before she changed her mind, he raced to his room. Two more words of the ancient writing. And she had written down at least some of her spells in English.

It wasn't difficult to fit the broken tablets together, to match the shapes and the writing. Here was the last part of *statue*—and here was the first part. Here was the first part of *patience* which his father had taught him; here was the end of *bravery*. Here was *stone*; this next sign could even be *peel* as his father had written on Harsu's own broken tablet. He should check that when he could.

In the first hour Harsu figured out it worked best if he peered at a few tablets, then moved to the parchments—there was far more pottery than parchment—then back to the tablets. Lists, recipes, spells. In a way any recipe was a spell, for turning what you wouldn't eat into something delicious. He rubbed his eyes. He had to concentrate. Sandstone—he might find out exactly how she turned people to stone.

The godlet-drops fizzed. What were the charm signs? How many of them were there, and in what order?

CHEAPEST SMARTPHONE

A GLEAM OF MORNING SUN CAME THROUGH THE curtain and Harsu woke. At the same moment, Daama poked her head around his door. She'd brought him a plate of ordinary toast with a smear of relish. She seemed surprised to see so many tidy piles already spread over the floor amongst the dust and fragments and pieces yet-to-be-glued.

"You're enjoying it? Keep at it then. I'll dash out for eggs." She still looked too weary for very much dashing.

The moment she left the house he hurried to fetch the cloak, arm-ring and lentil from the landing.

In case she changed her mind and came back at once, he thrust it all under the bed and picked up another tablet. *Sandstone*. Many other signs he couldn't read. But now *statue*. He sorted through the parchments and found one that looked as if it might match. *Sandstone, create, unmake. Bind.* But this sign …

Was Daama back? No. He fished the cloak from under the bed and checked the lentil against the tablet he'd found yesterday. Yes. The sign had to be *peel*, from his father's fourth line.

As he worked he heard Megan and her father. Loud. Arguing. He opened his window a crack.

"I hate you!" Megan shouted. "I want Mum!" A door slammed. Next he heard her angry tears in the garden.

Harsu tried to ignore it. It wasn't all his fault.

But in the end he slipped over the windowsill and through the long grass to the hedge.

"Megan?" He listened. There was a rustle further down the other side. He eased along. "Megan. I'm sorry."

"I hate you too," said her voice.

Well—good. Now she'd stay away.

Why should he care what happened to her and her family? He knew now that his mother did love him. She'd written his name. She'd made the handsome room for him. She wanted his help.

Harsu took a stride back to the cottage.

Then something made him stop. He waited.

"Dad won't believe me," said Megan's voice.

He turned around. "You can't blame him. My mother made him believe her."

Megan made a sound of anger. "So get me some proof I can show him. Proof of what I saw underground."

"If I do that my mother will hate me," said Harsu.

"Yeah," she said. "It's tricky as."

"Tricky because of the little kids and Ragnar," said Harsu.

Another pause. "Too tricky, eh," she said.

Another rustle. She was moving away.

Chin high, Harsu began back to the cottage. There in the branches of the lemon tree was a strange brown fruit. He froze. It was the claw-top. But it stayed silent and motionless. Stuck. Somehow he knew he had conquered it.

"Megan," he said. "I'll tell you everything."

Harsu found a gap in the hedge they could talk through. "It will take a long time," he said.

"Hunker down so I can see you properly," said Megan. "Start with that donkey-horse thing."

At last he'd finished. "It's true," he said.

Megan frowned. "As far as I know, there are zebras in zoos in New Zealand. But no onager."

"The war-steed is under New Zealand," said Harsu.

"Do war-steeds like apples?" she asked.

"It hasn't seen a fresh one for ages," he said. "Why?"

"Hang on." She ran off and was back in a minute. "Here." She tried to push a paper bag through the gap. "It won't go. What's the matter?"

"It's a barrier, like the gate. I just told you," he said.

"Far out," Megan muttered as if it was hard to believe

even with evidence right before her. "Okay. Stand back and catch."

A paper bag came flying over the hedge. He caught it easily. Inside were three green apples.

"Take them to the horse-thing," Megan said. "They'll keep it still while it's eating. Then here, use my phone to get proof. Catch again!"

He missed this one—the rectangle she kept in her pocket. But it landed safely on the long grass.

"Send me some pics," she said.

"What is *pics*?" he asked.

"On the phone," said Megan. "Shoot the onager. Shoot Ragnar in the jar."

"I won't hurt the onager," cried Harsu. "I can't hurt Ragnar!"

"Hurt them? Just take a picture! Oh …" Megan was silent for a second. "You don't know about phones and cameras."

"This is a good time to teach me," Harsu said.

Megan groaned. "Okay, I'll sneak Dad's. With luck he won't notice."

Harsu waited again. If Daama returned from the mini-mart …

But here was Megan again with a second phone. She lay down, looked through the hedge, held up the phone, then turned it to show him. On its glassy rectangle was a picture of a skinny boy with dark eyes and a scarred face. It must be a small mirror. He moved his head but the image stayed still.

"He looks like me. Who is he?"

"Shut up. Now take one of me. Hold my phone like this and press this button."

Harsu squinted through the hedge. "That's not a button. It's a very small picture."

"Image, button, icon, whatever," said Megan. "Dab it with a finger."

He fumbled with her phone. It wasn't quite the same as her father's. But at last he "shot" the hedge, then "shot" the dirt under it. Finally on the glassy screen he had an image of Megan through the leaves, her mouth turned down.

He glanced at the real Megan—she had half a smile.

"I am starting to believe you too," he said. "This is another great magic of New Zealand."

"It's the cheapest smartphone," she said. "Now as fast as you can, get a shot of the onager. Then some of the kids. It's really important to get a shot of Ragnar in that prison-jar." Her voice shook a little. "Also important, keep the phone on mute—don't touch this button. You don't want your mum to hear if it rings. And don't waste the battery on shooting rubbish."

"What is a battery?" he asked.

"All you need to know is this battery's down to twenty percent. Don't touch any other buttons … little pictures. When you're finished, throw my phone back over here. Okay?"

"Okay," said Harsu.

Leaves rustled as she disappeared again.

Harsu backed away from the hedge, brushed his hands through his hair to shake out telltale leaves and stray bugs.

The claw-top, dark as a dead fruit, stayed fixed in the lemon tree.

Patience is bravery. Harsu didn't think he had much of any other kind of courage but he spoke to the claw-top. "If I need you, I know where you are. Otherwise rot, for all I care."

SHOOTING AN EAR

A T THAT MOMENT THE GATE CLICKED. HARSU HAD NO
time to get back inside. He shoved the bag of apples
and the phone under his shirt and moved so his mother
could see him.

She had the trundler, full of eggs no doubt. "What are
you doing?"

"Taking a break," he called back. "Fresh air. Good for the
brain. I'm going in now."

He heard her chuckle.

As soon as he knew she was in her room he ran down
the wooden staircase, the slippery stone, on past shelves,
treasures, the looking-cakes stinking of pitch.

The sweet-water sea lay like moonlight. Copper leaves
clattered their faint tune.

Dgerr, he called softly, *dgerr.*

The onager stirred in the Ferry Gate. It shook the thick
black stripe of its mane and paced to him.

"Friend, I'm sorry. I've neglected you." Harsu held an apple on his open palm.

In two chomps the green apple had vanished.

"Don't move for a moment and I'll give you another."

Harsu took out the phone, pressed the little bar that made it glow and examined the buttons. It was like figuring out a new language.

At last he dabbed the screen. All he shot was the war-steed's ear.

He stepped back to fit in its whole head but it ambled up and nudged his chest.

If it loved him only for apples, Harsu didn't blame it. He placed the second apple on the ground and jumped back.

He managed to shoot the whole onager. He shot the Ferry Gate too. In case the onager followed him, Harsu lobbed the last apple far into the Gate.

Now to shoot Ragnar.

He sped through to the jar, whacked its side and aimed the phone. "Look up."

Ragnar groaned. "Any time I get comfortable you come and pester. I'm going to bash you."

"Bash me later." Harsu aimed the camera down the neck of the jar, then checked the phone. Good. Ragnar scowling.

He raced up, whisked through the kitchen—platters of nibbles lay on the table—and into the hall.

Daama's voice came from the front room across from her own. "What were you doing?"

"Using the wonderful bathroom." He slammed his door.

It was too risky to slip out his window again and throw Megan's phone back over the hedge. Daama kept moving up and down the hallway from that other front room. At one point he thought she'd disappeared to the cavern. But in moments she returned, groaning with physical and magical effort combined, Harsu guessed.

Then she was busy in the garden. He didn't go near the window in case she noticed and demanded to know why he wasn't at work. Besides, he was nearly halfway through the sorting and pasting. Learning too, he hoped.

The sun had begun to lower behind the hills when Daama finally called him.

Should he take Megan's phone with him? Yes. There could be a chance to get outside.

Daama wore a long skirt that covered her feet, a motherly apron as crisp as can be and her hair in a glossy bun.

She pushed him out the side door but stayed where she was inside the cottage. "I've no spare energy to manage the gate. You must stand there and hold it open. Make sure as many people as possible take a sweet-meat."

What did she have planned? Harsu stepped onto paving scrubbed clean by magic. In front of the cottage there was a lawn, fresh and green. Flowers in shades of blue stood ranked in beds. Surrounding shrubs were trimmed into shapely ovals. The back garden where the children had raced was far tidier than it had been, too, though the claw-top was still lodged in the lemon tree.

On a table inside the gate lay the platters of nibbles, like tiny cakes in cups of pleated paper, and little rolls of pastry. Beyond the gate was a waiting crowd. This was not good. Not good at all.

As soon as Harsu put a hand on the gate, the inrush of the crowd nearly bowled him over. Many people chose a sweet-meat. Some grabbed two or even three. A few held identical pieces of paper.

The man from the mini-mart was there. So were several people Harsu had seen riding past in cars. Grant was there with a tight hold on Megan's hand. The man looked stern and worried.

The crowd bunched near a new sliding glass window of that front room.

Harsu couldn't see over their shoulders. He reached for a crumpled paper in a girl's hand. "May I?"

She passed it over. He flattened it out.

"I can't understand all of it," he whispered. "Can you?"

In a light voice that stumbled a bit, she read aloud:

Counsellor for Family Contentment
Madam Daama, renowned specialist in child psychology
Established methods. Sure results.
Special preview
Enactment of notable triumphs

LIE UPON LIE

FOR SEVERAL MOMENTS HARSU COULD HARDLY BREATHE. What had he said to his mother? *People must see proof of your power. Thousands of men and women must learn from the mere sight of you.* She'd got a hundred, two hundred people here already. He'd only said it to buy more time. He'd got it so wrong.

The windows slid apart. In the room, a gauzy veil fell to show a platform with a grassy river bank. There stood Zamuna in his headband and linen kilt. He looked as proud as long-ago, but he seemed somehow artificial, not himself at all.

Now the little boy hung his head. His shoulders heaved. He clasped his hands over his chest and cried aloud.

"My mother and father disowned me because I was boastful and smug. Only a king may brag. Only a queen is allowed to boast. Only Madam Daama has been able to teach me how to be a modest boy."

At the load of lies Harsu's mouth fell open. The children in the crowd didn't look the least bit impressed. A few grown-ups paid great attention.

Daama appeared behind Zamuna. How kind she seemed, how protective.

He smiled up at her. "All praise and thanks to Madam Daama from this humble boy," he exclaimed.

In the garden the air blurred for a moment, and the plates of sweet-meats and good-meats passed around in invisible hands. As the platters emptied they refilled themselves.

Back in the room the platform revolved. A new scene showed Ragnar on a pebbled beach, as defiant as a warrior.

She'd let him out of his prison. For a moment Harsu felt hope again.

Then Ragnar slumped as if he were crestfallen.

"Shame on me," he cried. "I refused to obey my parents. I was so stubborn that they abandoned me." He wiped his nose on his arm. "I pleaded for them to return. My father shouted they were glad to see the back of me. My mother said my behaviour had broken her heart. Only Madam Daama has shown me how to be quiet and biddable. All praise and thanks to Madam Daama."

Daama appeared again and laid a hand on Ragnar's brow. He too smiled up at her.

This time several people murmured. "Interesting. How does she do it?"

A second time the platters of nibbles passed through the crowd. A second time the platform revolved.

The third scene was the forest. Blanche posed in her pretty dress, glanced over her shoulder and blinked with fear. Good acting, Harsu thought, or one of Daama's spells. No prize for the right guess.

Someone sighed. "What a dear little thing."

"I danced under the very nose of the Lord Protector," Blanche cried. "I shouted and sang. I was so rude and cheeky that my parents and all the villagers chased me into the forest. But there, Madam Daama saved me from the jaws of twenty wolves and a stampede of horses. Her kindness has taught me how to be meek and mild like a little girl should. What bliss it is to be obedient."

Harsu glimpsed children in the crowd roll their eyes at each other.

Daama glided to Blanche. The girl gazed at her with an adoring smile. "All praise to Madam Daama," she sang.

Silver cords drew the gauze curtain to hide the platform.

Some in the crowd were clapping and laughing. "This is a hoot." "Parents have always been at their wits' end." "Shut up and listen. It's ridiculous but it's great entertainment."

The people with half-eaten nibbles in their hands, however, sounded convinced. "Wow, the new super-nanny's our neighbour." "She's brilliant. What's her trick?"

Bells clashed and tinkled. On the platform Daama stood

alone, hands crossed on her apron bodice. When she spoke, it was smoother than cake-mix. "If any parent despairs, I understand. If your little ones refuse to go to bed, I can advise you. If they turn their noses up at the food you've slaved to put on the table, come to me. With all those annoying things they do, I promise to help. The first session is free."

More gauzy curtains fell over the platform, and the windows slid shut.

A late ray of sun dwindled behind the mountains. Several people left chuckling, others with suspicious shakes of their heads. But many were lingering, nibbling and nodding.

Grant and Megan were still in the throng. Her lip was curled as if she thought the whole performance had been disgusting. In Grant's hand was a half-eaten sweet-meat. He took Megan's arm and strode with her for the front door.

Harsu tried to fight through. The crowd blocked him.

The big door opened. He heard Daama purr to Grant. "Welcome. How may I help?"

STOAT-DANCE

IN A MOMENT DAAMA HAD GRANT AND MEGAN INSIDE
the hall. She signed a fluttering *depart* charm at the
crowd. Then the door shut as soft as a breath.

People started surging out to Caddie Street. Harsu struggled through them and finally swung round the side path
to the porch.

In the dining room Daama and Grant were murmuring.
Megan sat at the table, her hands balled into fists. As Harsu
entered, his mother stood and ushered Grant outside.

"Get up." Harsu tried to pull Megan to her feet. Her eyes
were flashing with anger but she seemed fixed in place.

"Megan! I've got the proof on your phone, the pictures
of the onager and the prison-jars. Who can I give them to?
When does your mother arrive?"

She didn't—couldn't—answer but her eyes looked even
more furious. He wasn't sure of a charm that might free her
and didn't dare mess anything up.

He raced out again. His mother and Grant had gone.

He dashed to Megan's house, to a patio, then a wide front porch. Through the open door he heard Daama's voice, and stepped in.

A big living room. Daama stood in the middle. She was whispering now, some long chant like the wail of a distant wind.

On a sofa Grant lay with his eyes closed, hands clasped on his chest.

Daama glanced at Harsu with a small smile. The chant lost a beat. But her fingers stayed busy in swift, delicate movement as she plucked a million grains of dust from the air, compressed and moulded them. Grant's face looked sandy, hardening already.

"You can't," said Harsu. "Not Megan's father. I haven't sorted the tablets, the parchments—you said you're not sure of the signs."

"He's a mere human man, why should you care." She continued the chant.

Grant's breathing became more shallow, his skin more and more like the surface of a statue.

The night deepened. There was no light in the room, no moon outside.

At last Daama's hands fell still. She bent to peer at the statue. It looked as if it would take the most shallow of breaths at any moment. "That will do."

Now she strode out.

Harsu refused to think of his father's form lying in the thicket. He clenched his jaw to keep back any sound of grief or rage. Right now he had to make Daama really believe he was her ally.

He turned and paced out to join her.

Megan still sat at the table, hands clenched and motionless. Daama gestured. The door to the landing flew open to show the three prison-jars. With a thud a fourth stood with them, rocking a little.

"No nonsense." Daama made a sign to free Megan's limbs. "Perfect girl, climb into the jar."

"I won't." Megan's words were no more than smothered breath.

"I've said it once, I won't say it again." Daama lifted a hand.

"It's illegal … Mum's coming back …"

"I spit upon any human mother." Daama scratched a sign.

In a whirl of air, Megan disappeared. The fourth jar rocked once more and the landing door slammed.

"Before the girl knows, she'll be out again. Harsu, I know you're worried. But come, I'll reassure you."

He followed her to her room. She beckoned him in.

Lamps sent out golden light over the best of her treasures. They crammed every inch, reflected again and again in many mirrors. Daama stood in front of the largest and wrapped herself in a fine linen robe. She fastened a gold necklace around her throat and put on a gold headdress. Her eyes glittered.

Heavy curtains over the high windows began parting to show the empty lawn.

"I promised you everything would be different in this place and time. It's coming true sooner than I believed. Watch me rejoice."

Arms wide, Daama began a low chant. The robe quivered and crumpled to a heap on the floor.

She had vanished.

But the chant continued under the robe. It grew into a growling. The growling rose in a shriek. From under the folds of the robe sprang a stoat.

Every muscle was sleek and strong. The fur glistened, thick and beautiful.

The stoat shrieked again. The windows slid open to the night.

Out the creature bounded into the dark. Around the garden it leapt, vaulted into trees and down again, spinning so fast it was almost a blur. A dance of joy, a dance of triumph, a snarl, a shriek. It turned itself in a circle, tail to snout, a ball of fur and claws that threw itself back up a tree.

A flurry of branches, a squawk, and a bird sped from the tangle of leaves. Some feathers floated about but the bird had escaped.

Down from the tree sprang the werestoat. "No eggs," it snarled, "I crave a warm egg." It slunk back and forth, low to the grass, tail lashing.

At last it paced towards Harsu ...

Then it was his mother in the linen robe again, human size but still half-stoat, reflected from every angle in the hundred mirrors. The necklace nestled around her furry throat.

She was waiting for him to speak. It had better be praise.

"Mother," Harsu said, "nothing you do could astonish me."

She chuckled. "And I have promised, you will be as me."

As her? "Actually—you said I was ready to grow."

She leaned forward. "That is true."

He nodded. "Good. So I'll be a man. But you have to let Megan out ..."

She gave that annoyed laugh he'd heard even from human mothers. "Harsu, one thing at a time. I said you were ready to grow. You will grow to be like your mother. To be a werestoat."

His knees nearly collapsed. "That's not what you said!"

A dangerous gleam showed in her eyes. "No child ever listens properly to its parent."

He wanted to shout *Did any parent ever speak clearly to its child?* "I won't be like you," he said. "I have the godlet-drops. They lift me up."

"*Ptah.* Every human child has at least one drop. It's up to each to decide if godlet-drops help them become good or bad."

"My father was human. He was good," said Harsu.

"Don't let that worry you." She chuckled again, though those eyes were still dangerous. "What's good for some is bad for others. My son will choose the way I have chosen."

"But not a werestoat! They—they stink."

"The best smell of all. Honey, *ptah!* I spit upon honey." She clapped her hands. "Now you must understand the pressure I'm under. Dealing with Megan so soon—but how could I pass up the chance? And that father of hers—I managed but it was a strain. Nevertheless, my son, right now you are the most important thing to me. I will prepare the Ceremony of the Werestoat."

The—what?

She continued. "It must be at New Moon—the dark of the moon—when I'm at my strongest. Can you bear to wait till then? It's a whole three days."

Three days. In three days she'd turn him into a werestoat. How could he stop her? He had to run now, this minute. He'd survive somehow.

But if he did, what would happen to Megan—to the others?

He tipped his head so she couldn't help but see the scars on his cheek. "Mother, look. I can't be a werestoat. I can't stand beside you. You know I'm not perfect and I never will be." But a breath shuddered in his chest and words flew out—"Mother, why haven't you ever charmed them away?"

Daama touched his arm. Harsu felt the same drag on his whole being as he'd felt from the claw-top.

"If I charmed the scars away, it would be dishonest."

Never, never would he understand her.

"And don't you realise?" she purred. "At last I have a flawless solution. When you're in stoat-shape the scars won't show."

PART FOUR

★

TIME & STONE

COLLAR OF DEVOTION

HARSU EASED THE FULL TRUNDLER OF EGGS DOWN THE step of the mini-mart. He should hurry back to work on the parchments and tablets.

"Hey," Tark's drowsy voice came after him, "tell your mum she makes primo cupcakes."

Harsu waved, then pressed a hand over Megan's phone in his jacket pocket. There was no use asking Tark to look at it and do something, not if he'd had Daama's nibbles.

There'd been hardly any cars on the way to the mini-mart. Now there were none on the way back. Nobody else on foot, nobody Harsu could ask to take Megan's phone. The whole of Redbridge seemed to be under a spell. This afternoon the only sound was the clattering of wheels from the trundler. Harsu had ripped off the ribbons and bells.

Twelve dozen eggs this time—one hundred and forty-four.

Daama had called and called to summon the claw-top,

searched and searched with no success. She needed more raw eggs than ever to keep up her energy.

The Ceremony. If Daama managed to stoat Harsu, he'd be eating raw eggs as well. He nearly threw up. To defeat Daama completely was the only way. He had to use what he was learning, what he was teaching himself. It seemed impossible. There was only today and tomorrow. Then New Moon.

A car engine, loud in the quiet street, started somewhere ahead. A grey car he hadn't seen before backed out of Megan's drive. It slowed and stopped next to him as he neared his gate.

The passenger window sank open and the driver leaned over. The woman with curly brown hair—he'd seen her with Megan. He felt she was trying hard to hide the fact that she was shaking.

She glanced at the gate, where the sign read *Counsellor for Family Contentment, opening soon.* "Excuse me. You're the boy who lives next to us, right? Have you seen Megan today? I'm Chloe, her mum."

He shook his head. It was true, he hadn't seen Megan today. If he told any more of the truth, Chloe wouldn't believe him.

Would she believe the proof on her daughter's phone? Harsu put a hand on it again.

Then he thought, but Chloe must have seen her husband, on the sofa, turned into sandstone.

He abandoned the shopping cart and raced to Megan's drive.

"Hey," Chloe cried. Harsu heard the car door slam and footsteps running after him.

He reached the patio and shielded his eyes to see through the window.

Grant's statue lay hands on chest, just as Daama had left it. Then one of its hands lifted a little and fell again.

Daama hadn't got the spell perfectly right after all.

Megan's mother arrived beside him, frowning. She had a phone of her own in one hand. "You know something, don't you? What's going on? Where is Megan!"

"Grant is alive—half alive," said Harsu. "You may think he is simply not well, or ... or has eaten fermented grain but—"

"What on earth are you talking about? Please make sense," Chloe said.

"Then don't yell till I have finished," Harsu replied. He wouldn't give her the cellphone till he'd finished, either.

There on the patio Megan's mother pressed her lips tight together and listened. Harsu felt grateful for such an unusual grown-up. It was especially hard to explain the Ferry Gate.

"It's a true story. But you must think it's impossible," he said at last.

Chloe frowned. "Of course I do. But ... " She stopped.

Now he pulled out Megan's phone. "There are pictures."

She snatched it, pressed a button and shook her head. "It's out of juice."

He should have kept it in a bowl of juice? Megan hadn't told him.

Chloe lit up her own phone. "I'm calling the ambulance. I'm calling the police."

"What is ambulance?" he asked. "What is police?"

She eyed him. "An ambulance is paramedics who'll take Grant to hospital. Police is law and order."

"My mother spits upon law and order," Harsu said. "When she is at her strongest, even New Zealand magic will find it hard to struggle against her."

Chloe's frown deepened. "Harsu, all that's clear to me is that something totally strange is going on. I work with the police all the time. I know they won't believe you. Nor will the paramedics. I mean, Grant's face is rough and grainy but for heaven's sake, sandstone? Look, I'll plug in Megan's phone and see what it has. But you'd better go."

Harsu peeled a rotten layer off a fat onion and tilted his head to hear any sound from the street. It had been ages since he returned. How long did law and order take?

On the window-seat Daama dropped eggshell into a dish and licked her fingers. "What are you doing?"

"Oh—imagining that when I'm a werestoat I will look more suitable for serving someone of your great talent."

"You're good with words," she said. "I'll have you coach the children. They'll pay attention when you're a stoat."

Harsu peeled another onion. "So why didn't you turn into a stoat to coach them?"

"Oh no, they'd have been terrified," Daama said. "Teaching is much better when it's done with my love and kindness."

He squeezed his eyes shut. She made no sense.

"What's that look?" she snapped.

"It's all the onions," he said. "I wish you'd chop them by enchantment."

"Sometimes I do," she said. "And sometimes I spend my spells on more significant matters."

Like a chandelier and a coffee machine. "There must be a machine in New Zealand to do the chopping."

"Yes, a food processor. I haven't needed one because I've used you." She picked up another raw egg.

At last the growl of a big vehicle stopped out in Caddie Street. The police?

Even though he knew they'd fail, Harsu's heart jumped.

He heard *thunks* of the doors, heavy boots on the next-door driveway, then the lighter steps of Chloe going to meet them.

Daama set the egg back in the bowl and slunk to the porch. Harsu ran out beside her.

In half a minute the boots crunched again. A woman and man in dark uniforms appeared at the cottage gate.

Before they put a hand on it, Daama raised hers palms up. She signed a charm Harsu hadn't seen before.

Four explosions burst in the street. The police ducked.

His mother glided to the gate. Harsu reached it before her.

The wheels of the big police car had become pools of black slop. Steam twisted from the grille at the front and spurted out the back.

Daama made another series of signs. An echoing voice spoke inside the car. *Bring the complainant in to the station, bring the complainant …*

While Chloe and the police climbed in, Daama drew forgetting charms and drowse charms. Even with its ruined wheels, the car lurched off in spurts of steam. The street stank of enchantment.

Daama stroked the good side of Harsu's face. "My magic is far more powerful than anything here. I can create any number of wonders. And when you're a werestoat, but in boy-shape of course, I will dress you to look a much more suitable son and servant, the kind I deserve. *Hmm …*"

She touched his scars with the tip of a finger. Whatever she was thinking now, he didn't like it. She began gliding back to the cottage.

"A werestoat is human sometimes … of course that's the point of it," she murmured. "Still, if I could … *hmm …* the Ceremony of the Stoat could be a much easier version.

But the enchantment is irreversible. Then again, I'd need only the collar of devotion, not the leash of loyalty."

"What are you talking about?" asked Harsu.

She reached the porch, turned to him and clapped her hands. "I have decided. Don't worry, my darling. There's no need for you to be a werestoat. You can just be a stoat. Then the scars will never show and you'll be perfect always."

QUAGMIRE

HARSU SAT CROSS-LEGGED ON HIS BEDROOM FLOOR. Every moment was like the worst taste ever. Two more days to save Zamuna, Ragnar and Blanche. If he didn't, he'd be a stoat for ever more.

On one side of him lay the tablets of pottery, all glued and sorted. On the other lay the sorted parchments.

A smear of paste remained in the pot. He reached for the cloak and fumbled the pieces of pottery lentil out of the pouch. He grabbed the brush and glued the halves together.

Patience is bravery. Things had only grown more and more terrible.

Wits are the best sickle-sword. His father's wits had not saved him from being turned into a statue. Harsu's own wits had not freed him or the stolen children.

The last line—*Time and stone peel away.* He supposed that was true. In the end, wind, rain, the burning sun and the cold of night eroded everything.

He looked at his own childish writing on the lentil's other side. *Harsu my son.*

Writing and reading hadn't helped at all. It had just showed him the breadth of Daama's power.

He raised the lentil to smash it again. But it would be more satisfying if he waited till the glue hardened.

Just a bit more patience, then. One half hour.

There was no choice now. He'd have to escape on his own.

Admit it, he told himself, admit you're a failure.

Now he didn't even want to escape. He'd be no use anywhere.

He bundled the cloak to hurl it away. One of the discs dug into his palm. He tore it right off and …

He could read the sign on it. It was for the setting of bones.

He grabbed the cloak and looked at the next disc—for the lowering of fever temperature. The next was for the spreading of honey on a wound to dissolve infection.

Then there was a blank disc.

The tokens after that looked as if the marks had been scratched with a dagger, maybe, or a surgeon's knife. Perhaps his father or the Chief Cook had made them.

Harsu looked more closely. Among the marks were: *my son.*

The rest of the faint signs on these few tokens began to make sense.

Fever She is angry I cannot cure my son Give him the lentil

It took a moment for the meaning to sink in. His father had known what Daama would do to him. But he had stayed with his son anyway, even run back to write this last line.

Harsu crouched again over the pottery tablets, over the parchments. No wonder Daama hadn't taught him to read. Reading was power that nobody could take away from you. Writing was power.

He'd got things wrong so many times. This time he had to be sure he got them right. Slowly he went through the tablets and parchments again. He could read signs for *claw* so easily now he almost laughed, and the signs for *spinning*. The claw-top. He'd been its master when he hurled it away and it had obeyed him.

A few days ago, so much that was written had been a maze before his eyes. Harsu had understood only single words, short phrases, sometimes a line or two at a time. Now his eyes were sending the meaning of the signs and letters straight to his brain. His eyes had learned their own magic. That's what his father had meant—his true power was writing and reading.

The godlet-drops burned with determination as he realised he could read and understand each one of Daama's charms.

While Harsu read on now, a plan started to form. It was crazy and it was logical.

"Thank you," he murmured to the Wind God or whatever god there might be. "Thanks for my own carelessness in dropping the crate and breaking the tablets. If I hadn't, Daama would not have decided to rewrite them and I would not have seen them."

When a warrior took a vow he got to his feet. Harsu stood and murmured aloud: "I put the words *if* and *maybe* and *cannot* to the sickle-sword. I will not run away. I will not be turned into a stoat. My mother will see that I am indeed a quagmire for her bedevilment."

WEAK SPOT

THAT NIGHT DAAMA SLEPT EXHAUSTED FROM ALL HER enchantments. In the gloom of the landing, Harsu signed the wake spell over Megan's prison-jar.

She struggled up, elbows on the rim. "I can't tell you how mad I am!"

"Hush. I need your help." Swiftly he told her what Daama had done to her father, to the police and her mother. Even in the dim light he saw her eyes grow wide and shocked.

"But there's a way to trap Daama," he continued. "Are you with me?"

She gestured to the prison-jar. "Like, I have an option?"

"Hear my plan," he said. "It has two steps. What does my mother feed on? She feeds on praise. So first we praise her as never before."

Megan closed her eyes and took a deep breath. "That is going to hurt. But go on."

"The stolen children—that includes you—have to say how

sorry you are for treating her badly. You must tell her she's the most wonderful, so on and so on."

"Tell lie after lie," said Megan. "What's second?"

"Second, I have to make her show her true self. To do that, we keep showing our false selves. Help me persuade the others to play along."

"But before the first step she has to let us out," Megan said. "That's the hardest."

"Not when you know her weak spot," said Harsu.

Harsu slipped out into the night to gather the claw-top from the lemon tree. "Thank you for staying hidden," he said to it.

Then back on the landing he roused the stolen children to stand up in their prison-jars. He held the wooden top to keep them silent while he explained his plan.

"And this, her claw-top, answers to me now," he told them. "Do you swear to follow the plan and work with me?"

"It means we have to lie about how wonderful and amazing Daama is," Megan said at once. "But it's called acting, right? And …" her voice nearly broke … "I have to save my dad."

Ragnar shrugged. Zamuna frowned. Blanche looked worried.

"I'll explain it again," said Harsu. "I make her believe there's a better way to impress the people of Redbridge.

Then we rehearse it underground. Because down there I can trick her into a prison-jar. I'll jam a stopper on it and she's trapped."

He waited a moment.

"You still don't look sure. Then let me do this …" Harsu brushed the air with a gathering sign that brought back memories.

"Oh …" A glisten of tears showed in Blanche's eyes. "My dough-nurse and I used to make simnel cake."

"I think she means yes, she's with us," Megan whispered to Harsu.

"My parents would have rowed back the next morning and found me gone," Ragnar said in a low voice. "I'll never see them again. But why not help Megan return to her parents?" He gave a sudden grin. "Yes. Adventure."

Zamuna's hand lifted from the rim of his jar and clenched into a small fist. "I am the best at acting. I am best at being a warrior who obeys the battle plan. I will be an honour to my parents." He thumped his own chest and bowed at Harsu.

Harsu bowed back. "Now the claw-top stays out of sight. Daama must not know I have it."

Megan eyed him. "So. Now you have to get Daama to agree."

"True," said Harsu. "We'll go over everything. Then I have to prepare some things in the cavern. Like a stopper of pitch."

Zamuna whispered, "Make it the best."

BRATS BEYOND BRATS

HARSU WOKE IN HIS WONDERFUL BEDROOM, IN HIS soft bed, under the coverlet patterned with stoat-prints. He had breakfast as usual, showered, which still felt unusual, and dressed in the comfortable clothes of New Zealand, cargo pants and a long-sleeve T-shirt.

Then he drew the arm-ring out of hiding. He pressed it to his forehead.

"Father," he said. "I've waited. Now it is time."

He pushed the arm-ring high up past his elbow and tucked the sleeve of the T-shirt under it to keep it in place. Next he put on a sweatshirt. The arm-ring was safe.

The plan he'd made was firm in his head. It had to be. There was nothing else to rely on. He knew Chloe had come home again but an ambulance had never arrived.

He went to his mother, on the window-seat with a box of jewellery. On her lap was a gold and lapis choker. She was fixing its buckle and didn't glance at him.

"What do you want? I've no time for foolery."

"This is the last morning before New Moon," he said. "The children are sorry. Show how generous a mother you are. Let them make peace with you."

"That is foolery." She held out the choker. "Try this."

He turned it over as if he admired it. "What a collar! My own triumph comes near. Mother, a son should support his parent and I have many ideas." He turned the collar again. "That performance the children did for the crowd was very good. But they did it under enchantment. It would save you so much energy if you didn't have to waste it on keeping them under control."

"Harsu, stop chattering. Try the collar."

He held it near his eyes, gave a cheeky smile and let the gold sparkle. Daama chuckled.

Now he tried the choker around his neck—too small of course—and kept his eyes twinkling. Daama laughed aloud.

He grinned back. "And another idea. If we have a second show even more perfect than the last ..."

"There is no improvement on perfection." She was still smiling though.

Patience, he told himself, *don't rush this*. "Very true. The first show proved your power over children. Many people were definitely convinced by it. But not everyone. So I wondered, what would happen if you added your other astonishing talent to the show?"

She began to speak but he talked over her.

"It would need just a flash of your magic. In New Zealand they call it *special effects*. They love it. It would take a lot of energy, but it would repay you a thousand times. The audience would be so frightened and astonished that you'd have control of the whole village. What next, who knows?"

Her eyes widened, narrowed again, then grew even wider while he kept explaining. Then …

"Oh." He bit his thumbnail. "No. There's a problem."

"Keep going," she said.

"There's no time to rehearse," said Harsu. "It has to be today because New Moon is tomorrow. I don't want to bother with the children while I'm preparing for the Ceremony. Afterwards I can't help the way I do now, because I'll just be a stoat. I don't want to wait a whole month for the next new moon. Never mind. It's all definitely off to a good start for you."

He tried the collar against his throat again and tipped his head in I'm-so-handsome. "One more day, then it's mine," he said, and let it drop back into his mother's hands.

Daama examined him. "You say the children are truly penitent. Very well, you may bring them to me. And your new idea is worth considering. Special effects, you say. Tell me again. If there is a problem, the favourite descendent of the Wind God will solve it."

—

The stolen children filed into the living room and stood under the chandelier. It sparkled even though it was daytime. They bowed to Daama.

"The mistress-princess is the most admirable mother in the universe," whispered Blanche.

"We have been brats beyond brats to the mother of mothers," Ragnar said.

"Five billion tears cannot show my sorrow." That was Zamuna.

Megan kept her eyes lowered. "It's a big responsibility being part of Daama's collection. I seriously want to live up to it."

Daama glanced at Harsu. He angled his head to make sure that she saw the scars on his cheek. She frowned as he expected. Then, as he hoped …

"Explain your idea to the children," Daama said.

THEY OBEY ME

IN THE UNDERGROUND MAZE DAAMA LED THE CHILDREN past the shelves with the wrapped looking-cakes, then reached the barrels, jars and flasks of all sizes.

"Look, here are some as small as Zamuna's handsome toes," said Ragnar.

"You must not tease today," the little boy replied solemnly. "We are here to show Daama how good we are."

Ragnar hung his head. "I apologise."

"Forgiven," Zamuna said.

"Very good," Harsu told them both. "Now, we'd better use the biggest barrel. This is the one."

"Is it vast enough?" asked Blanche. "Daama shouldn't have a single moment of being cramped and uncomfortable. I'd feel so guilty if she got the least little bruise."

"She's not going to fit, even in the biggest barrel," Megan said.

Daama chuckled. "Dear child, do not underestimate the

great-granddaughter of the Wind God. I'll decide on the best container."

"I'd better not help with the pushing," Zamuna said. "If I get a bruise too, it will wreck my perfection."

"Shut up, wimp," said Megan. "It's fake pushing, anyway."

"We must all join in," Blanche told him. "Just as when we all made that mess with the three looking-cakes."

"I feel so bad about that." Ragnar clamped a hand over his mouth.

Don't overdo it and don't laugh. Harsu gave him a secret kick.

But Daama's eyes had shut in self-satisfaction. "I was right to have hopes for these children," she murmured. She glided to the barrels. "This one is the biggest and we will use it."

"How are we to heave you into it?" Blanche asked.

"It doesn't have to be difficult, only seem difficult," Megan said. "Good acting."

"We need to rehearse a few times," said Harsu. "Mother, are you sure you'll be all right? Here, let's tip it on its side. There—that will be easier."

Daama examined the barrel.

"Now imagine this is the next Family Contentment show. To start with you'll be facing the audience with the barrel behind you. Yes, Mother. That's good. This first time through, I'll say the words, shall I?"

He cleared his throat. "You say to the crowd, *If children*

refuse to obey you at once, do not worry. That is normal. It happened once even to me. But behold the power and resilience of a strong parent. Then you kids, the moment she's finished, start acting. Try that bit now."

Behind Daama the children began to shriek at each other, kicking and punching. Daama turned towards them with open arms. Blanche and Megan took her hands and led her to the barrel. Zamuna and Ragnar helped her climb in.

Harsu crashed imaginary cymbals.

His mother backed out and spread her arms wide.

"And now they obey me every time," Harsu cried.

Megan wrinkled her nose. "That won't fool anyone. Where were the special effects?"

Daama looked at her with a sharp tooth showing.

"Not to be cheeky," Megan said. "But I do know about modern humans. I've been one for years."

"Yes, we forgot the stopping spell," said Harsu. "And, now Megan's mentioned it, the barrel's so big it looks far too easy. All four of you have to pretend to shove her hard."

"I never could, not shove Daama," cried Blanche, though her blue eyes sparkled.

"My dear, the point is," said Daama, "that it must seem difficult."

Which was exactly what Megan had said only moments ago.

"That's right, Mother," Harsu exclaimed. "The more

difficult it seems, the more wicked the children look. Then the more powerful you look when you break out, cast the stopping spell and they all stop dead."

On cue Ragnar agreed. "It will look amazing."

Harsu rushed on. "So Mother, remember the *halt* charm as soon as you're out. Nobody's a good enough actor to fake what it does to them. That's the special effect. Let's try again."

"This time, I'll say the lines." Daama flexed her shoulders and raised her voice. *"If children do not obey you at once, do not worry. It happened once even to me, Madam Daama."*

The children began their sham tantrums. Open-armed, Daama rushed to them. They screamed and pushed till she was in the barrel. Out she backed, turned and signed the *halt* spell. The children froze.

"Perfect." Harsu hated the spell. But it was the only way to make her so sure of the children that she wouldn't suspect the rest of his plan. And then he really needed her to do the stopping charm. "Say the last line, Mother."

"And now they obey me every time!" She made the release sign.

The children stumbled, dazed, Megan especially. Harsu feared that the plan would go wrong, but Blanche grabbed Megan and steadied her.

The plan kept on track.

"Please say we didn't hurt you, Daama," begged Blanche.

"Daama's a great warrior woman," Ragnar said. "She can withstand far more than human brats could do to her."

"She looks so beautiful when she casts the halting spell," Zamuna said. "Everyone would long to be the child of such a mother."

"Yeah, but it still looks fake to me," said Megan. "It's a shame she can't do it with a prison-jar. It would be terrific."

Harsu laughed and grabbed a small clay pot off a shelf. "Of course she can't. Next you'll say my mother should do it when she's a stoat. In a pot like this."

Blanche giggled, Ragnar roared and slapped his thigh, Zamuna let out a squeal of mirth.

"Yeah, right," scoffed Megan. "That would impress the crowd if she could do it. Biggest *if* ever."

"I have said, do not underestimate me," Daama began. She pointed to the line of prison-jars she had made for children yet to be caught. "We will use one of those."

But suddenly Blanche pointed to the shelf behind the jars. "There is my own doll!"

She leapt for it and shouted at Daama. "It's my own poppet that danced with me in the forest. My aunt helped me to make it and you threw it away. Then you stole it! It is not your poppet, it is mine!"

Harsu was a fool beyond fools. How he wished he'd remembered to fetch the doll. At the last minute, everything was ruined.

UNBREAKABLE

HARSU EXCHANGED A DESPERATE GLANCE WITH Megan, another with Ragnar.

Daama's look of scorn could have peeled onions. "What I find is mine. It stays mine always."

Megan dropped to her knees and whispered to Blanche.

The little girl's face screwed up with tears. But she kept them bitten in hard. She gave the doll a kiss, then carried it to Daama. Without a word she offered it up.

Daama took it.

Blanche curtseyed and swallowed before she spoke. "May my favourite doll never leave the hand of the mother to end all mothers."

Would that be enough to pacify Daama? Harsu managed not to shake. The stolen children were pale and tense.

At last Daama smiled. "Now," she said. "Where were we?"

"The jars," said Ragnar. "You wanted to try one."

From the corner of Harsu's eye he saw the stopper of

pitch he'd made and hidden earlier. It was still soft, as big as a head but shaped like a cake.

"No," he said. "My mother will not go in a prison-jar. As your son, Mother, I order you. No."

"You, order the most-loved descendant of the Wind God?" Daama cried. "Behold! Admire!" Her arms spread wide, though she still held the doll. She began a chant.

He hadn't meant her to do it so soon. He'd hoped for another rehearsal—but swift as a stoat, lithe as the wind, she was into the prison-jar.

Harsu dived, grabbed the stopper in both hands and jammed it on.

The stopper quivered. He could feel Daama trying to turn inside the jar. There was no room. Even so, she was snarling the *halt* spell to loosen the stopper. He battled her spell with a reversing charm he'd learnt from the pottery tablets. The halt sign would end up working only on her. And she'd boasted the urns were unbreakable. He'd caught her.

Harsu kept chanting.

But there was the sharp sound of a crack. A line zigzagged down the side of the jar. Another crack—he tried to counter it with the sign for *mend*—the sign for *bind*—

But in seconds Daama stood, shards of earthenware around her, the poppet under her foot.

"You said the jars were unbreakable—" Harsu began.

"I lied," she said.

PEEL AWAY

Daama's hands lifted as they had when Harsu saw her steal dust out of the air and turn Grant to sandstone—as they had when he was six, ill in bed, and he'd seen her do this to his own father.

"Run!" Megan shouted.

The children scattered—Blanche rushed down one path, Zamuna in the opposite direction, Ragnar for the underground sea.

Harsu flung himself for the stairs.

"You're a coward!" Megan yelled after him. "Save the little ones!"

"I'm no use if she catches me," Harsu shouted back. "Come on!"

"You said you'd use the claw-top to make sure of her!"

Not yet. He knew what he had to do first. Get proof, by getting a witness. Two witnesses would be even better. And if the jars could be broken …

Up the stairs he ran, faster than ever before. The arm-ring held firm on his upper arm. He leapt over the porch and hurdled the gate. Megan was beside him as he raced down her driveway.

Thank goodness, Megan's mother must have heard them coming. She was at the door.

For a moment it seemed she couldn't remember who Megan was.

But Megan cried, "Mum!"

Daama's forgetting charm broke. Chloe flung open her arms and Megan rushed into them.

"Where's Grant?" gasped Harsu.

"Mum, tell him quick," said Megan. "Where's Dad?"

Chloe pointed to the living room. There Grant lay on the sofa, one arm by his side, the other on his chest.

For a moment Harsu closed his eyes to remember what he'd seen—what he had read.

The godlet-drops felt buoyant in his blood.

He stretched out his arms. His fingers began the same fast movements as his mother's hands. But he added reversals, unwrapping signs he had learned from the pottery tablets and from his mother's copies in English. The dust in the air, heat of the air, cold of the air, the breath of the wind, the smoothing of water—*time and stone peel away* ...

Grant's hand flexed at his side. His head turned—the other hand reached to his eyes—they opened—

Harsu kept his fingers turning as if he spun an invisible top, peeling away the covering of dust and grit. The yellowy shade of sandstone faded from the man's face. Grant still looked pale but he was awake.

"How did you …" Chloe sank to her knees beside her husband. "Harsu—thank you!"

"It's not over yet." Harsu raced out again.

Now at least Chloe and Grant must believe his story.

And he was finally sure what would stop Daama for all time.

STOAT-DRIP

HARSU RACED DOWN THROUGH THE MAZE AGAIN AND slid to a stop on the silver pebbles. Beneath one of the trees stood Daama, fingers flying as they turned Blanche into stone. Zamuna lay nearby. But his skin was normal, his arms outstretched. She'd pinned him only by a sleep spell.

Where was Ragnar?

Megan's voice was calling for him. Behind her echoed the voices of her parents.

Harsu pulled the claw-top out of his jacket.

"Be still!" he roared, and flung it at Daama.

Her eyes widened in shock. The hum of the claw-top was louder than ever, the whirling more dizzying. But she managed to step forward, spread her arms to gather some tremendous effort—

"Fire, smoke and blood!" Ragnar jumped from a silver tree. He bowled himself at Daama and tumbled them both to the edge of the underground sea.

The claw-top circled the pair of them.

In two leaps Harsu was there. He guided the top away from Ragnar, then forced himself to send it hurtling to pin Daama more tightly while she was stunned.

A glance—Megan was kneeling next to Zamuna. Chloe and Grant were bending over Blanche. Ragnar was speeding to join them as if his young warrior arms would be protection.

Harsu began the movements over Daama that she had just been working on Blanche. He kept his chanting constant, near silent so it couldn't alter the flow of air needed to make the spell permanent. His mother's eyes were horrified to see he was so powerful.

The look turned to fury. She began her own chant—the one he'd heard when she transformed into a stoat. Harsu had to complete his charm before she finished hers. He kept pulling dust from the air, the smallest fragments of the silver sand under the pebbles on the underground shore, grains of shell and stone from the sweet-water sea, pushing them, moulding them to cover her.

The claw-top kept her trapped, but Daama's chant became a growling and rose in a shriek. Suddenly she was half-stoat, the eyes black pinpoints fixed on Harsu.

The godlet-drops filled him with increasing certainty. The memory of his father gave him strength. His friends needed him and he kept going. The coating of sandstone grew and thickened, the shape of the stoat took Daama over more slowly—one human hand remained—the head was all stoat—she still saw him move …

The arm-ring loosened and slipped down to Harsu's wrist.

Daama's eyes grew even more terrifying. Harsu's hands ached. The claw-top hummed, unceasing.

The crust of stone continued to form.

Slowly the fur of the stoat lost its shine. The creature seemed to hunch lower with the weight forming over it, the casing of stone that would preserve it forever. One last glisten of stoat-drip on its nose and tongue—

And it was finished.

The claw-top fell on its side.

Now Harsu made the sign for *bind* and the one for *eternity*. He took a step forward to make absolutely sure the stoat was motionless. It broke his heart to see it. His heart broke again when he thought it was too late to help his father.

But he sprang to Blanche and touched her cheek. It was warm but rough—part-sandstone. He wasn't sure he had strength left in him but he had to try.

"Watch the stoat," he gasped to Ragnar. "In case the reverse spell on Blanche has some effect on it."

He didn't think it would. But then, he'd only learned how to do any of this in the last couple of days.

Gently he began work again, coaxing the grit and powder

of stone to peel away from the little girl. At last she seemed free. But she just lay there.

"Do your swear-dance for Megan's mother," said Harsu. "I think she'd like it."

Blanche giggled. Megan reached to help her up.

"Let's leave Zamuna here," said Ragnar in Harsu's ear.

Harsu laughed and jabbed him with an elbow. Then he signed *wake* and Ragnar heaved the little boy to his handsome feet.

Megan's parents had watched speechless. Now Chloe gathered the two little ones to her.

Grant wrapped his arms around Megan. "Harsu, I can't find words to thank you properly …"

A little shakily Harsu walked nearer the stoat-statue. He looked up at the Ferry Gate and found the onager watching. It nodded to him.

Harsu had to stay in charge a little longer. "Sir, and Megan's mother, the children need to be cared for. Water. Something to eat."

"Of course," said Chloe. "Grant, let's get them to our place. Come on—" she smiled at Blanche and Zamuna—"we'll clean you up."

Ragnar hooted. "He can be the cleanest boy in the universe."

Zamuna grinned. "I'm faster than you anyway."

He darted off.